Junction

Time's Ticking

L. A. Evans

'Junction – Time's Ticking' by L. A. Evans
Published by Elizabeth Guttridge in 2020
LAEvansBooks@gmail.com

Printed and bound by Amazon

First Edition

ISBN: 9798663377652

L. A. Evans

For Olivia & James

Prologue

My index finger on my right-hand twitches. It sends a shiver through my rigid body. I can't move anything else. Open your eyes, I tell myself, but I can't. I hear faint voices around me but can't make any sense of their conversations. My senses are confused, but I can smell a strong scent of both antiseptic and lilies. I hate the smell of both.

My mother used to swear by TCP when I was a child. If I had a cut, an insect bite, a spot or a sting, the TCP would come out of the white, dusty bathroom cabinet. Adults look back to their childhoods and fondly remember the smell of things that made them better as a sick child. Like the smell of hot, mouth-wateringly sweet chicken soup, or crisply browned whole meal toast and honey, cut into soldiers. TCP, however, haunts me. The smell, the look and the anxious anticipation of when it hits your skin, making it viciously sting. Mouth ulcers, how I dreaded getting a mouth ulcer, as my mother would insist on making me gargle the disgusting stuff, saying, 'Aisha darling, open up, hold it for five seconds, and spit'. Gross.

The smell surrounding me grows stronger and makes my stomach churn and my head pound. Oh my head. Pain sours through me as my mind crawls back to the land of the living. The pain feels like a thousand daggers delving into my bruised and battered skull.

The stench of lilies always takes me back to the funeral of my granddad. My parents, Luke and I all sat at the front of the church, to say our goodbyes. The coffin was directly in front of us throughout the service, encased in white, stinking, lilies.

My granddad was the best grandparent a girl could wish for. I used to beg my parents every weekend to go and see him at his home in Birmingham. A two-and-a-half-hour trek from our home in Taunton was not something my mum and dad wanted to undertake every weekend. But the times they said yes, my heart would beat ten to the dozen with excitement at seeing my Granddad. Every time we would arrive at his house, he'd pick me up, whirl me around his head, and as he put me down, he'd plant a sharp, bristly kiss on my forehead.

He would play lots of games with me. He would play with my dolls, making up all sorts of soap opera dramas with them causing me to roar with laughter. He would take me out into his garden and play hide and seek, taking an age to find me. I'd always hide in an old wardrobe he kept in his garden shed. He never let on that he knew where I was every time, normally by the time he counted to one.

At the age of eighty-one, he died in his sleep. I miss him terribly.

The pain is travelling now. Every time I breathe in, my chest feels like there's a sharp piece of glass wedged in my rib cage, cutting into my lungs inch by inch. My thighs throb as if I've run a marathon, aching and pulsating throughout my lower torso. I think the only parts of my whole body that don't cry out with pain are my feet.

I can hear people talking and rushing around me, but they may as well be foreigners. I can't make out a single word. I try to open my mouth to say something, anything. But my mouth is sealed shut. I am so thirsty.

I have never felt thirst like this before. I remember once, I was on holiday with mum and dad in Cornwall, and we went out for the day to a small cove on the south coast. It was a blazing hot summer's day and my parents interrupted my car sleep to drag me out for a walk down to the cove.

With map in hand, my dad led the way, saying it'd only be a ten-minute walk. Every few minutes I'd ask if we were nearly there, and every time, I'd get the same response, that it's just around the bend. I hate walking at the best of times, but this went on for what seemed like forever. About fifty minutes later we finally reached the cove. Mum asked if I'd like an ice-cream when we reached a van on the edge of the beach. An ice-cream was the last thing I wanted, I needed water. Mum bought me a bottle of ice-cold water, and I'll never forget the cleansing, quenching taste of that Cornish drink.

That was nothing in comparison to how I feel right at this moment. My mouth tastes and feels rotten. I try to move my tongue around to get a build-up of saliva going. My teeth have grown fur and my tongue seems to occupy my whole mouth. What precious saliva I introduce back to my mouth reaches my tongue and I swallow. It even hurts to swallow.

I move my index finger again. The voices around me grow louder and clearer, I hear the words, 'She's waking up.'

A man's voice whispers in my ear. 'Love? Can you hear me? It's OK, love, you've been in a car accident, you're in hospital, but you're going to be OK.' I'm not alone, Luke is here with me and I feel him take my hand.

I process his words. A car accident, I don't remember being in one. I vaguely remember seeing Mrs Wyatt. But that's it. I can't respond but at least Luke is here, and he'll look after me. Everything will be OK. With that, I fall back into a deep sleep.

Part 1

1

A year ago

My six o'clock alarm buzzes. Today is the second of June, my big day when I become Mrs Aisha Brown. Gemma, my best friend, stirs in the bed next to mine, yawns and jumps onto my bed, waking me with laughter and excitement. My mother slowly opens the bedroom door, armed with two cups of coffee and asks me if I've looked out of the window yet. I look out, and the sky is a glorious blue, with no clouds in sight. This is what I'd prayed so hard for; perfect weather on my perfect day. Things couldn't look brighter.

I first met Luke at a party. I was the last one to arrive of course, all flustered, red faced and out of breath. Gemma was celebrating her twenty-fifth birthday and invited some of her work friends along, as well as the usual crowd. Luke works with Gemma at the same primary school, but Gemma teaches older children between the ages of nine and ten.

I noticed Luke's beaming smile as soon as I bounded through Gemma's living room door. I mean, who wouldn't? Dark, flowing hair parted to one side, bright blue, sparkling eyes and ice white, perfect teeth gleaming through his upturned lips. I hesitantly smiled back at him, spotting the only vacant seat, next to him on the sofa.

'You must be Aisha,' he beamed at me. 'I've heard a lot about you from Gemma. What you go through in your life. Gemma's constantly taking time off work to look after you, isn't she?'

'Hmm, so she's still making up stories about my life in order to pull sickies, then is she?' I said.

'Well, it's either that, or your pet dog's died three times, you've suffered from flu about fifteen times and your boyfriend always cheats on you.' He continued.

I paused, smiled at him and said, 'I think I'm going to have to speak to Gemma again about my duties as a best friend. I'm not quite sure being a constant excuse for her to skive off work is one of them. I don't, and never have had a dog - they smell, I've had the flu jab as I suffer from asthma, and currently I don't have a boyfriend - and that is not because I've been cheated on umpteen times!'.

'Well, I can tell you now, if you were my girl, there's no way I could ever cheat on you.'

I blushed, heart pounding I said, 'If you were my man, I think I'd be using Gemma as an excuse for me to skive off work to be with you.'

From that moment on, we never left each other's side. And to this day, Luke never lets me forget how forward and corny that line was.

Luke proposed to me over a three-course meal he prepared for me on Valentine's Day last year. Luke has always been a romantic man, showering me with gifts over the years, from flowers to weekend breaks, he really knows how to make me feel special. We'd been together for six years, lived together for four, and last year, he finally plucked up the courage to ask me to be his wife. From that moment on, it was planning.

Sixteen months of planning table arrangements, choosing dresses and accessories, arranging vendors and the day has arrived. The last year-and-a-half I have been the most organised I have been in my life. Everything has been planned to the tee. I have a running order for the photos at the church, for the venue, for the speeches, for the evening do and importantly for the morning of the wedding. For once in my life, I can't be late. This is it; this is the start of my magical day and there's not a moment to lose.

At breakfast I am ravenous. Not even the nerves of a wedding can suppress my appetite. I eat a bowl of cereal, two croissants with butter and honey, four slices of bread and drink two cups of strong coffee. Normally I don't take sugar in my coffee, but due to the nerves, I ask my mum to put a little 'taste' in my hot drink. On my fourth piece of toast, my parents interrupt my gorging, laden with gifts.

I open a square box first, tied together with a purple bow. It's a silver necklace with a beautiful diamanté encrusted cross hanging from the centre. My parents tell me it's my something old, a necklace they bought on the internet which is over a hundred years old. It really is beautiful.

I unwrap the next present from its delicate pink tissue paper and take out a brand new, stunning, ivory bag, with little pearls dotted all over it. It's the same bag as the one I spotted when I went shopping with my mother for make-up a month ago. She remembered.

The smallest gift contains a pair of pearl earrings, encased in silver. I remember these. They're my mother's earrings that she wore on her wedding day. I've seen them in my parents' wedding photos and can't quite believe she's still got them. I feel honoured to wear them on my special day and pray my marriage will be as long lasting and loving as my parents'.

Staring closely into a mirror, I put in my contact lenses and start to pile on the make-up. I don't normally wear much make-up. I usually just apply a little foundation to try to hide the freckles that cover my face and some mascara. But today, I apply everything. I coat my face in the expensive foundation I bought especially for today. To make my hazel eyes look bigger, I apply dark brown liner along some false lashes. Finally, I sweep a little blush underneath my cheek bones in the vain attempt to look like I have some.

Gemma helps me into my white, strapless dress that glitters with ivory gems. My dark brown hair is curled and delicately piled on top of my head, with long curls flowing down my chest. My hairdresser recommended this style to suit my heart-shaped face. Set in between curls are little sparkly silver and pearl clips. My mother stands behind me and places my full-length veil at the base of the clipped back curls. I am good to go.

I wave goodbye to Gemma and my mother as they leave to go to the church, and glance at my dad. He can't take his eyes off me, and his eyes fill with proud father-of-the-bride tears. 'You look absolutely beautiful Aisha,' he says. It's taken until my wedding day, to finally be at peace with the body that I've hated for so long.

Everything has run smoothly, from receiving the most gorgeous pink-and-white bouquets to the vintage cream-and-black wedding car arriving on time to fetch me. But the car has to wait. We have fifteen minutes until I should be walking down the aisle, and I remember I don't have my something blue. I turn to my dad and ask him what I can do. This is the last thing I need on my wedding day. I can't go through with it until I have my something blue. There is nothing blue in the house. My dad is great, he searches everywhere. I try to help him but one, I'm incredibly stressed out so I can't see for looking, and two, I am wearing a huge white dress with four-inch heels which hinders my searching.

My Dad comes out of the kitchen with something in his hand. He gives it to me and says that he's sure this will do the trick. Outside, I hear the horn of a car. It's time to go.

We squeeze into the back of the car and set off on our journey to the church. The church is in Monkton Healthfield, the next village away from mine. The car pulls up to a crossroads, the locals call the Camel Hump. A cold shiver runs from my neck, down my arms, to my fingertips. My dad squeezes my hand, sensing my body jerk and tells me everything will be fine. But it's a strange sensation. It's not about the wedding; I know that will be fine. I love Luke and I want to spend the rest of my life with him. This shiver is like someone looking over me, protecting me. From what, I don't know. It's like a warning.

I look at my dad, sat next to me, full of pride. I forget the feeling I just had. I have no doubts about my life with Luke. Instead, I fill my body with the feeling of excitement and squeeze my dad's hand, telling him it's just around the bend.

I turn up at the church fifteen minutes late with a piece of blue tack lodged between the sole and the heel of my ivory wedding shoes.

The vicar looks rather annoyed, but I'm so wrapped up in everything that's happened, I barely notice the grimace forming on his face. Gemma greets us both with a concerned expression. I tell her about my something blue drama and show her the underneath of my shoe. She chuckles and breathes a sigh of relief. She tells me that Luke looks very handsome in his wedding suit and that he's waiting patiently for me.

With Gemma binging up the rear, my dad takes my arm and walks me towards my soon-to-be husband.

There are at least seventy guests filling the church. Most of them I know and some of them I don't. Although, I'm sure by the end of the day, I will. There are some people missing though; namely my late grandfather who passed away two years ago. I would have loved nothing more, than to have him here with us today. In my heart, I know he's here, smiling down on us and wishing us both all the happiness in the world.

Luke has his back to me as he waits patiently at the altar and I saunter down the aisle feeling like the most beautiful creature that ever walked the earth. All I see is Luke. Nothing else is brought into focus. As I reach the altar, he turns to face me with tears in his eyes, and murmurs, 'You look gorgeous.' For the first time in my life, I do.

As I look into Luke's eyes, I know right then that saying yes was the best decision I ever made. He stands there looking every bit the handsome man I fell in love with. Dressed in a dark grey suit, with silver and pink waistcoat and matching pink tie, he really does scrub up well. His dark hair is neatly combed behind his ears and his piercing blue eyes are filled with glistening tears.

We say our vows with every meaning; for richer, for poorer, in sickness and in health, until death do us part. We are pronounced husband and wife and I kiss my new husband. Luke takes my hand in his and the congregation applaud as we walk down the aisle to Mendelssohn's Wedding March. I glance at Luke and his smile is exuding happiness. However, the same shiver as I experienced in the wedding car tingles down my spine. Adrenaline pumps through my veins making me want to flee. Something isn't right. Suddenly feeling conscious of my troubled expression, I swallow the inexplicable feeling of dread, force a smile and focus on my friends and family cheering and whooping.

I have never doubted my relationship with Luke before or questioned our love for each other. Yet, I cannot shake this feeling that something terrible is going to happen.

2

Yesterday

It's been a long, hard shift at work. My last client for today is my least favourite, Mrs Bishop. Just the thought of seeing her makes my breast ache. I place my hand over the scar hidden by my uniform.

A couple of months ago, I was subject to her favourite pastime, biting. Minding my own business, helping her get comfortable in her bed one evening, I tucked her into her copious blankets and stroked her head, whilst whispering good night in her ear. The next thing I knew, her teeth embedded themselves into the soft flesh of my left breast. She wouldn't let go. I swallowed the pain, tears pooling in my eyes and forced out the words to tell Mrs Bishop that it hurt. Through gritted teeth, I told her that this was unacceptable, and that she wouldn't get any help from me in the future, unless she released me. I caught her eye, looking up at me through her bald eyelashes; she winked at me and released me. With that, she rested her head and fell fast asleep.

Today she's on her best behaviour. She still complains that the pillow I give her is too lumpy, the water I pour her is too cold and her nightdress is creased. But all in all, she is good as gold, no biting sensitive areas.

It's now eight o'clock in the evening and I'm heading home. This morning I told Luke I'd be home at seven-thirty, but half-an-hour late is progress. All day I've looked forward to walking through my front door, as today is our first-year anniversary.

I reach the driveway of our new home, park my car and walk up to the front door. The door is unlocked as usual, so I walk into our hallway. I'm greeted by large, pink, paper hearts in a trail on the floor from the front door into the lounge. I drop my handbag by the front door and, with a stupid childish grin, follow the trail. The lounge door is slightly ajar and excitedly I open it. Luke has laid out a summer picnic blanket in the centre of the lounge, with a whole array of tasty treats spread out to make my mouth water. Luke is sitting on one cushion with an empty cushion by his side. He taps the top of the empty one, ushering me to sit down next to him.

I take my seat and give him a long kiss. As I pull away, I mouth the words, 'Thank you'. In response, he smiles and mouths back, 'No problem'. All my favourite food is set out in front of me, including sandwiches, savoury snacks and a variety of beautiful little cakes. He cracks open a bottle of bubbly, and pours us both a glass and toasts, 'To us.'

After munching my way through half the food set in front of me, I'm on my third chocolate crispy cake and he says, 'Aisha, wouldn't it be great if this time next year, we had a little son or daughter to make our family complete?'

This is a conversation we've had many a time over the last few months. The one thing both Luke and I so desperately want is a baby. I don't really want this conversation now, as every time we talk about it, it ruins the mood. You see, we've been trying now since the wedding, and I just can't get pregnant. I've learnt all about the menstrual cycle, timing exactly the best time in my cycle to conceive, I've upped my exercise (I actually walk to the corner shop instead of drive now), I've even made Luke wear boxers rather than tight underwear. But to no avail.

I know we would make fantastic parents. Luke is a primary school teacher at our local school, just outside Taunton, and he is brilliant with the kids. He teaches five- and six-year-olds and they love him. As a care worker, I love to look after people and I honestly believe I am particularly good at what I do. Clients always ask for me over other staff members, apart from Mrs Bishop (but then she doesn't like anyone). We both enjoy looking after other people's family, but we want our own to look after.

I smile a sorrowful smile at Luke and say, 'You know that's what I dream of, our own family, but I don't know what else to do.'

'Perhaps we need to seek professional advice,' he says.

'I guess you're right, it's been too long now. But let me go to the doctor in my own time.'

The thing is I'm terrified. I'm terrified that it's me, my body, that's stopping us from having a baby. I can't bear the thought of never being a mother, of disappointing Luke, of preventing our parents from becoming grandparents. I know it takes two to tango, and it could be Luke with the fertility problems, but deep down I have this nagging feeling that it's me.

'We'll go together,' he says. 'We'll have the appropriate tests and at least we'll know Aisha, and I'm sure we'll be given some options and help'.

'You're right,' I say. I know he's right, but I just can't face it. Not at the moment, when everything is going so well between us. We're married, we've got great jobs that we love, a new house in a lovely village, and I just don't want anything to put a dampener on our lives. But what if there's nothing wrong with either of us? That would be fantastic news; we'd just need to give it more time. But I can't stop this nagging thought, that it's me. 'Let's give it one more month, and then we'll go, I promise.'

*

It's been five minutes since I last looked at my watch. I'm with Mrs Wyatt, a sweet old lady but a complete chatterbox. Born and bred in Somerset, she's lived the busy life of a farmer's wife and mother, now grandmother, and now she's confined to her house, like a prisoner. Normally, I chat away with her but today I have other things on my mind. She notices

I'm quieter than I normally am and asks, 'Usually I can't shut you up Aisha, what's up with you? Probably be summut to do with that there husband of yours, I know that look, and it's definitely a man's doin'.'

'Oh Mrs Wyatt, no it's not Luke, it's just I've got a very important appointment later today and I keep thinking about it,' I reply. 'Sorry, I've been terribly rude, I'm here with you so let's get you fed, you must be starving, and it's almost twelve-thirty.'

'What are we having then today dear? Are you joining me?' she asks. She always says this every lunchtime shift I work with her. It really is endearing.

'No, no, Mrs Wyatt, you know I'd love to, but rules...'

'Are rules,' she finishes my sentence. 'Well then, you make some sandwiches and then you can tell me all about this here appointment that's got you all pre-occupied and worried.'

I make Mrs Wyatt her favourite sandwiches, cream cheese, ham, tomato and lettuce. I pick at the ham as I make them, I can never resist. As I chew on the meat, I glance around her kitchen. It really is quaint. A little dusty due to less maintenance nowadays, but everything is in its place.

I bring the sandwiches into Mrs Wyatt's lounge and place them on her little table in front of her armchair for her to easily reach and enjoy. I take a moment to look at her. For an eighty-three-year-old, she really is remarkable. She's frail, and can't walk well, but she's incredibly with it. Her silver perm is neatly combed, she's dressed in her Sunday best, as always, and her nails are neatly painted in her usual bright pink. I imagine her as a young lady; she would have been incredibly beautiful at one time.

As Mrs Wyatt tucks into her lunch my eyes drift to the photos on her mantelpiece. I can count at least six frames on the mantelpiece alone. There's a photo of Mrs Wyatt and her late husband, side-by-side smiling at each other rather than at the photographer. It must have been taken a number of years ago as Mrs Wyatt doesn't look much older than seventy in it. There's a beach in the background, it looks like Weston-Super-Mare with the donkeys trotting past on the sand. They're on a bench and each hold a whipped ice-cream in their hands.

There are many photos of children. Two are old black-and-white photos showing three children, two boys and one girl. There are two coloured photos of other children, which I can tell are still old as they are fading and dusty.

The largest photo is in the centre of the mantelpiece and it's of a group of people, with Mr and Mrs Wyatt in the middle. It must be a family photo, perhaps the last one Mrs Wyatt had taken with everyone in it, including her husband. It looks like three generations, all together for one big family portrait. I feel sadness but can't help but smile at Mrs Wyatt standing in the middle, proud of the big happy family surrounding her.

'So, Aisha,' she says, snapping me back to the present. 'What be causin' you all this concern and clock watchin'?'

'Mrs Wyatt, you have children and grandchildren, don't you?'

'Oh yes, I got three children and seven grandchildren. I also got a great grandchild on the way!' She smiles as she says this.

'Congratulations Mrs Wyatt,' I say batting back the tears forming in the corners of my eyes. 'I didn't realise, that's wonderful news.' I honestly wish her every happiness.

Mrs Wyatt can sense the sadness in my tone and says, 'What is it me dear? There's summut troublin' you.'

'Well, it's a bit personal and I wouldn't want to trouble you with it.'

'There'll be no troubling my lovely. Who am I gonna tell?'

'Well,' I say. 'I'd love a family of my own one day but we're having a few problems you see … I'm going to see the doctor this afternoon to get some test results back.'

'Oh, don't you worry about that, me dear, a fit young thing like you, you'll be fine. Is Mr Brown goin' with you to get 'em?' She sees me shake my head and continues. 'Well, I ain't havin' you goin' alone, you need someone to go with you. Now get me out of this chair and I'll come along dear.'

'I would love the company Mrs Wyatt, but I can't take you out of the house. You know, rules are…'

'Rules', she sighs. 'Well, you go there, and you hold your head up high. These days there be so many things them doctors can do for you youngsters now. Back in my day, there were none of this IBF and whatnot. You'll have your family my dear. All the good 'uns get what they deserve in life. You and Mr Brown are good 'uns, and you'll get your family.'

'I hope so Mrs Wyatt', I reply. 'And if I have half as many beautiful family photos on my mantelpiece when I'm your age, as you do, then I'll be one lucky lady.'

I wash her dishes and make sure she's got plenty of water in her glass, on her table. I say my goodbyes and clock off. I head to my car and think about what she said. Yes, we deserve to be parents; life wouldn't be that cruel, surely. I'm sure I'll be fine. For the first time since the initial appointment two weeks ago, I feel positive about hearing the results. Thanks, Mrs Wyatt.

I haven't told Luke. I didn't want him to come with me, as I really didn't want him to be there when the doctor told me it was me, that I was the reason we couldn't have children. But as I get into my car, I want him to be with me so badly. I feel guilty. He deserves to know what's stopping us from conceiving as much as me. After all, it could be him; he could have fertility problems. How am I going to tell him I've done this alone, especially if I'm OK? One of us must have fertility problems and if it's not me... But I have to continue this on my own. It's no use asking him to come now. It's too late in the day to tell him now, I must face this alone.

*

The doctor's surgery is in a village, two miles away from Mrs Wyatt's house, on my way home. Inside every seat is taken apart from one. The woman next to me looks like the healthiest person here. And then she sneezes, three times in a row, and gives an almighty cough, I raise my eyebrows, and think *typical*.

A young nurse enters the room and calls my name. This is it, the moment of truth. My knees are weak as I pull myself out of the chair. I look around me as I leave the waiting room and wonder what other people are waiting for. They could have serious illnesses such as cancer or heart disease. They could be depressed or stressed. I'm here awaiting results to see if I can have children. Perspective is a sweet thing, but it doesn't make me feel any better.

I enter the doctor's consultation room. Dr Bright awaits me. She ushers me in and asks me to sit down. She's a lovely doctor as she always makes me feel at ease. She can tell that I'm nervous and smiles.

'Hello Aisha', she says, 'I'm sure you're very anxious to know your test results, so I'm going to discuss them all with you one by one. Didn't you bring anyone with you today?'

I shake my head.

She frowns and continues to talk me through all the results. My heart sinks. She tells me that I have premature ovarian failure. My ovaries have stopped working. I have a five per cent chance of conceiving naturally and there is no treatment she can give me to effectively increase my fertility. She explains that I will need to undergo hormonal replacement therapy to reduce the risk of bone loss or osteoporosis. I zone out. I have heard what I came here to hear. My worst fears are confirmed, I am unlikely to ever have my own child.

*

How do I tell Luke? My head is a blur and it's pounding. I've returned to my car, and I can't cry. I feel completely numb. How could this happen to me, to us? What if Luke can't get over the fact that he can't have children with me? He might leave me, or if he doesn't, I'll always wonder if he will. I can't live without Luke; he can't leave me. But how do we move on from this? Finally, I let out a huge, heart retching sob and bury my head in my arms on the steering wheel.

I start the car, contact lenses blurred with tears, and head home. I turn up the volume on my car radio in a vain attempt to distract my overactive thoughts. Luke's going to wonder where I am, I was supposed to be home an hour ago. But I guess when I get home he'll know where I've been soon enough. I head towards my village and pull up at the Camel Hump crossroads. A song I've never heard before starts playing:

> *I've much on my mind and no way to turn,*
> *Should I go back or keep moving on?*
> *The hurt that I feel deep inside of my soul,*
> *Lingers inside my intrepid form.*
> *Oh, help me return,*
>
> *To my life before.*

I pause and listen to the words, as they sum up exactly how I feel at this moment in time. Suddenly a pain soars through me and I am plunged into darkness.

3

Present day

My index finger on my right-hand twitches again. It brings me back to the present and to the intense pain surging through my body. My neck aches, sending sharp, intermittent shockwaves up to my throbbing head. Can I open my eyes? I try. I open them ever so slightly, but the light is blinding. My hand is being held tightly, and my thumb stroked gently.

Though muffled, I can make out the words, 'That's it love, take your time, you're waking up, it's OK. I'm here and I'll look after you.'

Luke will, he always does throughout everything. He was there by my side during my granddad's funeral, never letting go of my hand. He helped me through the tough times when I had no job, when nothing made sense and I didn't know who I was anymore. He was the one who encouraged me to follow my dream of nursing, finding me the job in care work and supporting me as I took my diploma in health and social care. And he's here now, looking after me.

I move my tongue around the inside of my lips, trying desperately to moisten them. I manage to croak, 'Water'.

My voice sounds deeper and raspier due to the dehydration.

'Oh, of course love, I'll be right back.' Thank goodness for that.

I wonder if my mum and dad are here somewhere, or if they'll visit me later. My mum always makes me feel better. She has a way with words that always calms me down and puts me at ease. I guess that's what mums are for, always there, always helping you through the tough times in life, and sharing in the good times. My dad would cheer me up. He would probably crack some joke about me being typical Aisha, never one to do things by halves. He'd do or say something to annoy my mum, she'd glare at him, he'd cower slightly, and I'd laugh. I want to laugh now; I want to feel happy again. Please let them come and see me.

'Here you go sweetheart, slowly raise your head, and you'll feel a straw in front of you, but only take small sips, you've been asleep for an exceptionally long time.' Water, at long last, I listen to Luke.

He puts his hand underneath my head and coaxes me towards the water. I take the straw between my teeth and sip. The cold, fresh water is so delicious and refreshing. It instantly eases the pounding and rattling of my poor brain. I lower my head back down towards my pillow.

The water has helped loosen my tongue, so I ask, 'Where are mum and dad?'

I expected Luke to say they're on their way, or they'll be here later, but he doesn't. Instead, there's silence. The buzzing around me stops. And I hear whispering. I strain to hear what is being said.

'What does she mean by that?' My husband sounds shocked and concerned.

'She must be suffering from some confusion,' a man with an authoritative voice says. 'It's typical after what she's been through, but she'll come around. She's been asleep for a long time.'

'Love, I don't really know what to say,' Luke says. 'Your parents aren't here sweetheart. I know you would want them to be here with you, but you've got me. I've looked after you since they passed away and I'll continue to look after you. I won't let you out of my sight. Not until you're completely recovered.'

What? No, they can't be dead. I only saw them last week. What is he on about? I need my parents. I need to see their faces and hear their voices. I start to open my eyes.

I slowly peel back my eyelids. The room is a blur, whirling around me, I feel sick. My stomach turns over, and over again. The spinning of the room gradually slows down. A long fluorescent light comes into focus above me. No wonder I couldn't bear to open my eyes with this thing looming over my bed. I roll my eyes over to my right and a man in a long white coat stands by my bedside.

'Welcome back to the land of the living,' says the doctor. 'You had us all worried for a while there, but you're going to be just fine.'

I don't particularly feel fine, but at least I'm on the road to recovery now. I roll my eyes over to my left. My hand is in the firm grasp of a blonde haired, muscular stranger.

He smiles down at me and says, 'Thank god for that, hey love? If I'd lost you, I don't know what I'd have done. I love you so much, Zoe.'

I start to panic. Who are you? And who the hell is Zoe?

*

As I re-gain my consciousness, my hand is clasped tightly in the grasp of the blonde stranger who is looking intently at me.

'Who the hell are you?' I blurt out. I can't contain the confusion within me. Why is this man by my bedside? A man I've never met before who's claiming to know and care for me.

He looks hurt and puzzled. 'It's me Zoe. It's me. What do you mean who the hell am I?'

'Stop calling me Zoe! I don't know who you think I am, but I'm not Zoe.' Pain ripples from my legs straight to my brain. It's overwhelming. Both the pain and the confusion take control of my body and I shake violently. 'Get out!'

He doesn't understand me. He just looks at me with tears welling in his eyes. 'But I love you. You need me,' he says.

'I just need to be alone. Please, get out!' It's my natural response. I just want my family. I want them to hold me, to hug me and say everything will be OK.

The doctor takes the strange man by the arm and ushers him to the corner of my curtained room. I can hear the doctor saying to him, 'It's quite common for patients who have suffered head injuries to experience some memory loss when they awake from a coma. She's very confused. I think it best you leave her to fully absorb her surroundings and adjust to what has happened to her.'

The blonde-haired stranger looks at me with such pain in his eyes, but I don't care. I can see his pain, but I don't understand it. I just need to gather my thoughts and figure out what is going on.

'I'm not happy about leaving her,' the man says. 'She needs me, she may not know it, but she does.'

'What she needs right now is time and rest.' The doctor insists.

I see the man nod at the doctor, and he turns to me and says, 'I love you Zoe, I'll let you rest.' And then he leaves.

Relief floods through me. My anger subsides and I'm just left numb and exhausted. The doctor walks towards my bed, checks a machine to my side. He turns to me and says, 'You may be suffering from some memory loss. It's nothing to worry about at this moment in time. You've been through a tough few days and this is your body's way of dealing with it. You're on a lot of medication at the moment which can affect your memory. We'll re-evaluate the situation tomorrow, but if there are no improvements, I may reduce your medication. What I need you to do now Zoe is rest.'

He leaves. I am exhausted, but how does he expect me to rest after everything I've seen and heard. I feel lonely and frightened. What on earth has happened to me?

*

It's nine o'clock in the evening, so the clock on the wall tells me. I slept on and off for two hours. I didn't think I would, but my body needed it. The hospital ward is settling down for the night. For the third time, since the doctor left, the nurse comes to my bedside to ask me if there's anything she can get me. The truth is I don't want anything. I just want to be left alone.

The first time she woke me was to remove my catheter. I had it inserted whilst I was in my coma. She also checked the machine by my head and checked my notes at the foot of my bed. I also got the feeling she was checking up on me. She must know what happened earlier, as she had sympathy for me etched all over her face. The second time she interrupted my sleep, she brought me some water and pain killers. She again checked my machine and my notes, then scuttled off.

Now on the third wake up, when she asks me if there's anything that she can get me, I just shake my head. Yes, she could get me my husband. That would be a start. Then she could fetch my parents and my best friend. Finally, she could get me a taxi home. But I don't say any of these things. I just shake my head as what's the point?

Two hours ago, I opened my eyes and saw a stranger sat by my bedside. Two hours ago, I was called Zoe instead of

Aisha. Two hours ago, confusion and anger caused me to lash out at this strange man. Now I am left, feeling sick and lonely.

I try to process everything I heard since coming around from my coma. My parents are dead. Luke, Gemma, everyone I know, and love are nowhere to be seen. I wake up to see a stranger who knows me as a girl named Zoe. I have no idea who he is and who he thinks I am. He must be some sort of weirdo. How can the hospital let a weirdo in to see me? He must be off his head. Or so incredibly lonely that he has to prey on a vulnerable woman, waking from a coma, and pretend he's her husband.

I look around my small, curtained room. The asparagus green curtains completely enclose the space. There's a brown leather chair next to my bed on one side and a large bouquet of white lilies, set on a round metal cabinet, on the other. Next to the lilies is a big card saying *Get Well Soon.* I reach over, wincing through the pain in my ribs, and take the card in my hand. I open it, and inside it reads. *To my darling wife Zoe, please wake up soon, I love you and I miss you. Yours always, Tom x*

Tom. I think about the name. Tom. Who does he think he is? I rip the card up. As I do so, a glint of golden sparkle comes from my left hand. I scatter the shards of card onto the hospital floor and bring my hand closer to my face. I am greeted by a rock the size of a marble on my left ring finger. A gold band, with a singular diamond set inside a gold plate. A separate gold cut band lies comfortably underneath it. My nails are pristine. Shaped beautifully and French manicured, with little purple flowers set into the hard varnish. I turn the rings round and round on my finger, prising them loose. I put them in my left palm. I take the diamond engagement ring and hold it up to the luminous light above my head. It catches the light beautifully. I hold it closer to my face to study it. It reflects the green from the curtains. Why am I wearing these? Luke and I chose white gold for our wedding jewellery. Subtle crystals embedded in the silver bands. Not this monstrosity. That weirdo must have put them on my finger. But what's he done with my rings? I can't look at them anymore, so put them down next to the stinking lilies.

This must be some sort of a nightmare. At some point, I will wake up, and Luke will be sat on that brown leather chair, holding my hand, smiling at me. My parents will walk through the curtains, rush over to me and kiss my cheeks. Gemma will drop by with a pile of girly magazines, probably all wrinkled from last night's bath water.

I close my eyes and rest my weary head. I think about Luke. I think back to when our vicar gave us a book to read before our wedding. *Preparing for Marriage* it was called. It was book full of experiences and thought-provoking questions on all sorts of topics: arguments, religion, sex, children, sickness and many more. A number of questions we found very difficult to answer, but one was incredibly easy for the both of us. *What would you do if one of you left the other?* We both answered *that would never happen.* I laugh ironically.

I catch myself doing that thing I do when I'm thinking intensely about something. I'm sucking my teeth. Only, now my teeth feel alien. They are perfectly set in a straight line top and bottom. My crooked bottom teeth are now straight as an arrow. This isn't right. My mum begged me to get braces as a teenager, before I got too old, but I didn't want them. I liked the uneven look of my teeth. It was me. It was how I was made. Now they're gone and replaced with a dentist's dream.

The same nurse interrupts me again as she quietly sticks her head around the curtain. I open my eyes and glare at her. 'It's ten o'clock, time for your other set of pills,' she says.

She slides a table in front of me and stands a glass of water on it. She puts two pills by the side of the glass and urges me to swallow them. I take them in my hand and one by one, I feed them into my mouth, each pill followed by a sip of water. My bladder stirs. I need the loo.

'Can I please go to the toilet?' I ask the nurse.

'Of course, I'll bring you the bedpan,' she replies.

Oh no. I can't cope with the embarrassment of peeing in bed. I help people pee for a living. I make sure they're comfortable and do everything I can so as not to embarrass them. However, I do not want to be on the receiving end of this public humiliation.

'Please, no,' I beg. 'Can you help me to the bathroom, so I can have a little privacy?'

'Well, you're really not up to it and you shouldn't be walking so soon after coming around.'

'I can cope if you help me.' I say.

The nurse frowns and shakes her head in disapproval. She sighs. 'I can't do that; you need to rest. If you need to go, I must insist you use a bedpan.'

So, I swallow my pride, and allow the nurse to help me.

*

People buzz all around me. Daylight floods through the hospital ward. Trays of food and drink are being distributed to every patient. It's breakfast time. I have no idea how I did it, but I slept right the way through the night. The nurse left me at ten-thirty last night, I closed my eyes, and here I am. Awake at the start of a new day.

'Morning Zoe,' a cheerful, young nurse bumbles in to see me. 'I'm Donna, or on formal occasions Nurse Watson and it's time for your pills and bed bath.'

I thought I'd suffered enough humiliation last night with the bedpan, and now a strange overly happy nurse is going to wash my private bits.

She senses my embarrassment and says, 'Oh don't you worry my love. I do this all the time. You're in safe hands and it'll all be over in a few minutes.'

I know it won't take long. I've washed loads of clients over the years and I don't bat an eyelid when I do it. But when it's you that's being washed it's a different story. But I reluctantly let her wash me. I must admit, I could do with a freshening up, I feel absolutely disgusting.

As Donna gets to work on me, I say, 'I must look an absolute state, if I was in a coma for as long as the doctor said I was.'

Rolling me onto my side to scrub my back, Donna replies, 'Oh my love, I don't think you could ever look an absolute state. Someone like you, it'd take a lot more than a car accident and a two-day coma to stop you being the envy of most women!'

As she rolls me over, my hair falls over my face, I take a bunch of hair to tuck it behind my ear, away from my eyes. As I do so, I gasp. Since when did I become blonde? And I've had a haircut. This is the first time since being in hospital I've seen my hair. What on earth possessed me to bleach it? I went blonde ten years ago and hated it. It drained my complexion and the next day I went straight to the chemist to buy brown hair dye. Why would I do it? It doesn't make any sense.

'I'm blonde,' I shriek.

Donna says, 'Why yes love, it really does suit you. Beautiful cut as well I'm sure, if it were tidied up a bit. I wish I were as blonde as you are, not this mop of ginger madness. Some people say it's ginger, I like to call it strawberry blonde.'

I interrupt her, 'But I hate my hair blonde. I can't have been thinking straight when I did this. As soon as I'm out of here, I'm hitting the bottle.'

'Oh, it's not that bad love, you don't need to drown your sorrows with alcohol!' She winks at me.

I can't help but smile and let out a little giggle. I like Donna.

'I don't suppose, when you've finished, you could fetch me a mirror please? I want to see why I thought it was a good idea to go blonde.' I ask. 'I can't imagine it would suit me, but you seem to approve.'

'Of course,' she says. 'But I must warn you, you won't look like your normal self. You've been in the wars, so your face is slightly bruised and swollen in places. Let me at least brush your hair, before you go checking yourself out.'

Donna finishes up my bed bath and leaves to go and fetch me a mirror and hairbrush.

Again, confusion rears its ugly head. What is going on? I list the events of the twenty-four hours in my head. I wake up from a two-day coma with a strange blonde-haired muscle man named Tom by my bedside. He insists on calling me Zoe. In fact, the whole hospital insists on calling me Zoe. Since seeing Mrs Wyatt, I've straightened my teeth out, French manicured my nails and dyed my hair blonde. Unless, I did have a brace as a child, as my mum wanted me to, and forgot. Perhaps I did decide to change my looks, go blonde, I may have. Maybe that man, Tom, had my nails painted whilst I was unconscious, so that I felt better about myself when I woke up. Has the coma left me brain damaged or amnesiac?

Armed with a mirror and hairbrush, Donna returns. 'Right, let's get you tarted up for your hot date with the mirror then.'

Gently, she starts to comb my matted hair. She can't get through it completely. But she manages to comb the surface, tidying it up a bit.

'Right, are you ready?' she says. 'Don't forget, you do have some bruising and ...'

'It's fine. I understand. Please, hand it over to me.'

She gives me the mirror and slowly I raise it to my head. I close my eyes as suddenly I feel terrified to look. I have an awful feeling inside me that I'm not going to like what I see. I raise the mirror so that the light is blocked from my closed eyelids. It's right in front of my nose. I can do this. I gradually open my eyes.

Staring back at me in the mirror, behind all the bruising, is a chiselled jaw, blue eyes and a blonde bob. I am staring at a complete stranger.

4

'Are you OK my love?' Donna asks me. 'You've gone terribly pale. What on Earth's the matter? The bruising will fade, and you'll soon be back to your beautiful self.'

I can't even bring myself to answer her. I just stare at the face in the mirror. I don't see the bruising she mentions, only what lies beneath it. My eyes explore the reflection, from the widow's peak at the top of the forehead, down to the dimple in the chin.

The reflection's eyebrows are neatly trimmed, shaping the big, sky-blue eyes underneath them. The nose is blemish-free, not a freckle in sight. The cheekbones are prominent, jutting out of the cheeks like hidden blades. The mouth is supported by two full lips which are perfectly shaped and pink. The jaw is squared, jutting out at the sides.

My eyes travel down from the chiselled jaw to the neck which is set between two distinctive collarbones. There's a strange blemish on the right collarbone. It's brown in colour and the size of a fifty pence piece. It looks like a birth mark.

I touch my nose and the reflection does the same. I move my head to the side and again the reflection obliges. The blue eyes fill with tears, and I can no longer see. I hand the mirror back.

'There, there, lovey,' Donna puts her arm around my shoulder and gently rubs. 'Give it some time and I promise you the bruising will fade.'

'Oh no, no, no … it's not that.' I reply through sobs. How can I tell her I don't recognise myself? 'I just look so … different.'

'I know,' she says. 'I know. I don't like to leave you like this, but I have to go and see …'

'Don't worry,' I say. 'I'll be OK in a minute. I just have to adjust.'

She smiles at me sympathetically and leaves.

She's left the mirror on the table next to my bed. I leave it well alone. I've seen enough from that thing. I run my fingers through my hair, pulling strands in front of my face. What has happened to me? Why can't I remember who I am and what I look like?

Pulling my bed sheets down, I look down at my body. There's nothing to me. My stomach is flat, my hip bones jut out at my sides and my breasts are small and pert. I can't be much more than a size eight.

Putting my hands over my eyes, I start to sob. It's so confusing. It's not that I don't remember what I look like. It's that I remember myself as something completely different. Before the accident, I'd be lucky if I could see my feet whilst lying down.

I wipe my eyes in my hands, and as I put my hands down, I notice my arms. Why hadn't I noticed them before? They are so toned and muscular. I clench my fist and bring it up towards my shoulder. The muscles bulge and strain. I look at my left hand where those hideous rings had been and I now notice the veins and tendons protruding from it. The nails still look beautiful, but I can see now that my fingers are long and thin, like a piano player's.

The green hospital gown covers my body. I lift the neck hole to peer at my breasts. The small scar from Mrs Bishop is no longer there. It's like my memories are slowly being wiped away. I remember it so clearly; Mrs Bishop's teeth digging into my flesh, tearing through it and leaving their mark. Instead of a scar, I find a silver ring, pierced through my left nipple. The look of it makes me feel sick. I only ever had my ears pierced. I never saw why people would want holes put through any other part of their body. Now I have an unsightly ring embedded in my breast.

It only just occurs to me. I can see clearly. Am I still wearing my contacts, and no-one's noticed? That's not good if they've been in my eyes for all this time. I pick up the mirror and glare at the reflection glaring back at me. Pulling the mirror closer to my face, I search for my contacts. Prodding and poking my eyes until they turn bloodshot, I can't find any lenses. I have perfect vision.

What has happened to me? I keep asking this question repeatedly, but I can't make any sense of it. How can I have been living my normal life one day, crashed my car the next and then wake up as a completely different person?

I try to think back to the car accident. How did it happen and where was I going? Then a thought springs to mind. Was anyone in the car with me? No, I can't imagine I'd have been driving anyone. The last thing I remember was being at Mrs Wyatt's house. I certainly wouldn't have driven her anywhere. Was there another car involved? If so, I wonder if the other driver is OK. What if the accident was my fault and I've killed someone? I've been so wrapped up in what happened to me, I haven't spared a thought for anyone else.

The curtains move and the doctor comes in. I quickly cover myself in the sheets.

'Good morning Zoe,' he says, smiling. 'And how are you today?'

I smile back but I don't answer. He moves towards the bed, checks my notes and then the machine. He turns to me and notices the mirror which I've rested on my chest.

'Ah, been having a look at your war injuries I see,' he says.

'The nurse gave me the mirror so that I could see what happened to me,' I reply.

'Well, your injuries aren't as bad as they look, but I am a little concerned about your memory. You seemed very confused yesterday and I was wondering how you were feeling today.'

How am I feeling? If he thinks I was confused yesterday, then he's in for a shock when I tell him how I feel today. How do I tell him I don't recognise myself? I don't know who I am. I have no idea what's happened to me or what I'm going to do. I'm completely alone and can't begin to sum up how I feel.

'I don't remember anything.' That's all I can think of to say.

He smiles again at me. 'You won't remember anything about the crash yet. I'm sorry to say, you may never remember what happened.'

That's not what I meant. 'Actually, I meant I don't remember anything at all. I've been lying here trying to understand what has happened, but I just keep going around in circles. I don't know who I am.'

'Hmm… You've had a hard blow to the head Zoe. But I wasn't expecting a memory loss. Try telling me what you *do* remember.'

Where on Earth should I start? I remember being Aisha Brown, married to a handsome, wonderful husband named Luke. I had a mum and dad who loved me and a best friend who would do anything for me. Luke and I had just bought a house and I loved my job as a care worker. I was overweight, brown haired, hazel eyed and freckly, but I was happy. Now I'm skinny, toned and blonde. I'm alone with no-one to hold me and no-one to love me.

'I remember a different life. I wasn't who I am now. I'm sorry, I can't explain. You'll think I'm mad.'

I start to cry. I've cried so much since waking up that my eyes feel old and abused.

'Please, try to explain. I know it's upsetting, but I need to know how much you remember so that we can give you the help you need.' The doctor says.

I take a deep breath. 'Before the accident, I was happily married. Not to the man I saw yesterday, but to someone else. I wasn't called Zoe and my parents were alive. I saw them a week ago...'

I can't continue. It's too hard to say these things out loud. He won't understand me. He'll deem me insane if I tell him the full scale of my memories and send me off with the men in white coats.

The doctor looks concerned. He raises his eyebrows, pulls out a pad and makes some notes.

'I'd like to reduce your medication Zoe, you may suffer some more pain, but I don't think the meds are helping your memory. I'd also like you to see a colleague of mine. You can talk things through with her. She's called Doctor Read and she's a great listener. I'll bring her to see you later today. For now, I need you to continue resting.'

I'm not sure I want to know the answer to my next question, but I ask. 'Was anyone else hurt in the accident?'

'Yes,' he says. 'The driver of the other car suffered similar injuries to you. But she's going to make a full recovery, too. Don't worry about anyone else, just concentrate on yourself.'

'Oh, thank goodness. I was worried. I hope it wasn't my fault,' I say. He shakes his head. 'How long am I going to stay here for?'

'You'll be staying here until I'm happy that you're ready to go home, both physically and mentally,' he says and then he leaves.

*

My eyes are red and swollen as I wake from my afternoon doze. Going to sleep after an hour of continuous crying has not been kind to me.

I think back to what the doctor said. *You'll be staying here until I'm happy that you're ready to go home, both physically and mentally.* Does he think I am mentally ill? Perhaps I am. I'm a completely different person from who I remember being. He's right; I have had a major blow to my head. Is this what people with head injuries encounter when they wake with amnesia? Is this amnesia? Could it be possible that all my memories are fiction? Perhaps I dreamt my memories whilst I was in my coma. No, surely that's impossible. I have so many memories, not only of Luke but of my childhood and my granddad. There are too many to make up in two days. But there's no mistaking that I am ...

'Zoe?' I lift my head up and see a female doctor standing at the bottom of my bed. 'My name's Claire. How are you feeling?'

Why does everyone keep asking me that? I feel shit. This must be Doctor Read.

'I'm OK,' I lie.

'I understand you're a little confused since waking up. I'd like to help you, Zoe. But to do that, I need you to talk to me. Please, take things one step at a time.' She has a kind tone to her voice. She's not like the other doctor. It's not that he's nasty, but his authority makes me uncomfortable.

I need to tell someone. These thoughts are driving me crazy. That's if I'm not already. Its time things came out in the open. I need someone to tell me this is normal, that I'm going to be OK. So, I start from the beginning.

5

An hour ago, I told Claire everything. I told her how last week I was happily married to Luke and we were planning a family, how I met up with my parents every week and how I loved my job as a care worker. I explained that I last remember seeing an old client of mine and then I woke up in hospital. Since then everything has been a whirlwind. I look like a completely different person and now I'm married to a man named Tom who loves me, but I don't remember our wedding day, our relationship before or after. The memories I have don't seem to have happened at all. My whole life appears to be fantasy, replaced by nothing. I have nothing, other than the memories of a life that I'm told didn't exist.

She sat by my bed, let me talk and listened to everything I told her. She nodded at all the right times and scribbled notes down in her pad. Every now and then, she lifted her head to give me a confused, sympathetic glance, but always returned to her notepad.

This is what I needed since coming around. I needed to offload all these thoughts that have been buzzing around my head. I asked her if she thought this was normal after a head injury. She told me it's uncommon, but it does happen.

She explained that head traumas can cause memory loss. It is possible, that the dreams I had, whilst I was unconscious, replaced my memories. The trauma to my brain could have had such an impact that it wiped the hard drive of my mind and the dreams were copied and installed. She said she would do what she could to help find the lost data of my life.

Reassuring me, she told me that I shouldn't worry. Many people who wake up from a coma after a head injury suffer from memory loss of some sort and a personality change. It is possible that I regain my memory, but it is unlikely that my personality will revert completely back to what it was. What I need to do is begin to understand myself and rebuild my life. To do this, I need to be under close supervision and receive some psychiatric help.

As my physical injuries are healing well, she refers me to the rehabilitation unit in the hospital. This is to help me return home and prepare me to face society and everyday life. A team of health professionals who specialise in head trauma await me.

*

Two weeks have passed since I was moved to the rehabilitation unit. Tom requested to see me numerous times, and each time he asked, I refused to see him. I wasn't ready.

The team of doctors here have been so helpful. I have spent many sessions talking through my life and memories. They have helped me rebuild my confidence and mental strength. I haven't remembered anything about my life as Zoe, but I now feel ready to explore its possibilities.

I am due to be discharged in two days, so I have agreed to see Tom.

He is a striking looking man. He has a presence which turns heads. As he enters my room, carrying a large bunch of flowers, I turn to look at him and fully absorb his appearance.

He has short blonde hair with a spiked-up quiff at the front. His build is nothing short of massive. He's not fat, he's just incredibly muscular. He has a kind smile on his face which makes his cheeks dimple at both sides. He's wearing a V-necked T-shirt and tufts of blond hair curl out from his chest.

I am incredibly nervous to see him. All I can say is, 'Hi.'

'Am I pleased to see you!' He replies and smiles. 'These are for you.'

I take the flowers. They are beautiful red carnations. I lift them to my nose and inhale deeply. They smell gorgeous. 'Thank you.'

'I know lilies are your favourite but seeing as you had them whilst you were in hospital, I thought you'd appreciate the change,' he says.

'Yes, thank you, I do appreciate it.' Really, I do. I can't cope with the smell of more lilies.

He sits down on an armchair next to mine. He looks so nervous. I'm glad I'm not the only one. He tells me he understands what I've been through and that it will take time, but he'll help me to remember. It must be difficult for him. He knows me as his wife. He has all the memories of our life together, but I can't share them with him.

Through my therapy sessions, I gained a little more perspective. I was terribly confused and lonely and all I could think of was me. Why did this happen to me? What am I going to do? How do I get my life back? What the therapy has made me realise is that I'm not the only hurt person. Here is a man who has lost his wife. He can't grieve as she's still alive, but she can't remember him. She doesn't remember all the fun times they shared, all the arguments they had and the making up they did. I owe it to us to find out more about my life as Zoe and my marriage to Tom.

I explain to him it's not going to be easy. I will hurt him, not intentionally, but I will. I tell him I don't remember anything about our life, but I'm willing to try. There must be a reason why I married him, and I want to remember why. It will be tough, and I will get confused, but I have nowhere else to go. My life is with him so that's where I need to start in order to rebuild it.

The therapists explained to me, during rehab, that I need to familiarise myself with normal surroundings. I need to return to my normal life, with Tom, if I stand any chance of regaining my memory. Apart from my body, there is nothing in hospital that relates to my life before the car accident. I have nothing at all that relates to the life I thought I lived before the accident.

I still have all my dreams of Luke, my best friend Gemma, mum and dad. But I have realised, they are just dreams. There is nothing in my present that relates to them. What I have now is Tom. What I need now, is normality and routine.

'I'm being discharged in two days,' I tell Tom. 'Can I come and stay with you? Only, I have nowhere else to go.'

'Oh love, you don't need to ask,' He says. 'It's your home. I'm just so pleased you're willing to give it a try.'

Tears form in his eyes. I can see how much he cares about me. It's etched all over his face. I know he wants reassurance. He wants my love in return but that's something I can't give him.

I take a deep breath. 'I can't give you what you want yet Tom. I don't remember our life. I don't remember you. I'm sorry. But, with your help, perhaps I will start to remember.'

I feel so bad being so blunt, but there's no other way to say it. He's a complete stranger. My heart belongs to Luke, but Luke isn't real. I have to start believing that otherwise I won't move on. Tom's here and he's willing to love and help me.

*

My bag is packed. I don't have many belongings with me, only a few items of clothes, a toothbrush and some other toiletries. Tom kindly left them with me when I first woke up. I never really appreciated them until I moved to the rehabilitation clinic. I also have a small bag of Zoe's that was brought in with me after the accident. There's not much in there; some tissues, a purse with a few cards in and a stick of lipstick. A far cry from the Mary Poppins bag I normally carried with me containing hat stand and all.

I've had my final meeting with the doctors to discuss on-going appointments and monitoring. Now I am waiting for Tom to come and collect me. My nerves are building inside me.

Tom is about to arrive, to take me to a home I don't remember. Do I know the neighbours? That's if we have any. Do we have any pets? Do I have children? No, surely, they'd have prepared me for that. They wouldn't let me just turn up and play mother without giving me forewarning.

I give the staff at the hospital my thanks, take my bag in my hand and walk out of the main doors. I really can't thank them enough for what they've done for me. It's lovely to smell the fresh air and feel the breeze on my skin. I'm still hobbling due to the pain in my ribs, but all the other pain has ceased. The doctors said my ribs would take the longest to heal.

I've arranged for Tom to collect me from the main entrance as parking is always horrific at hospitals. On time, he pulls up in a shiny, new Mazda MX convertible.

Tom gets out of the driver's seat, takes my bag from me and opens the passenger door.

What am I doing? Panic rises in my stomach. I can't get in the car. I don't know this man. He could be a serial killer for all I know. My heart tells me this isn't right, but my mind tells me to trust him. He's all I've got.

'It's OK, take your time.' Tom places his arm around my shoulder. I flinch and he quickly removes it.

'I'm sorry,' I say. I can do this. Face your fears and get in the car. The doctors wouldn't let you get into a car with a psychopath. I slowly ease myself into the convertible.

The car journey is awkward. We sit in complete silence. But the breeze in my hair and the sun beating down on my skin is a glorious feeling. I put my head back on the head rest, close my eyes and absorb the rays.

The feel of wind in my hair and the sound of the engine purring beneath me remind me of the fun fair at Burnham-on-Sea. Luke and I go there every summer and ride the waltzers. We never tire of them. We ride them repeatedly until we're both green and vow we'll never go on them again.

I switch my thoughts back to the car. My therapist said that whenever I think of Luke or something from my dreams, I must bring myself back to the here and now. It's difficult, but I need to concentrate on the present. Luke is a past fantasy, a life I must forget.

I open my eyes and look over at Tom. He glances at me and smiles.

'I thought you were dozing off then, love,' he says. 'Do you want the radio on?'

I'd do anything to cut through this silence apart from talk. 'Yes, please.'

The radio plays some reggae. Not the usual thing I'd listen to, but I enjoy the beat and listen to it. I lean back on the head rest again and stare out of the window.

Where am I going? I wonder what our home is like. It's probably a standard two up, two down, terraced house. I hope there's a garden though. That's the one thing I asked for when Luke and I went house hunting. It's important to me to have some outdoor space but with little maintenance. I don't have green fingers, but I'd love somewhere private to sit on a warm summer's day.

We pull into a narrow lane. It winds all the way up a small hill. As we reach the top, I see the house. It's huge. From the front, I can count four windows top and bottom. A pathway, engulfed in a green sea of grass, leads to the front entrance. Tom slows down when he reaches a beautifully paved drive at the side of the house and stops in front of the garage. He holds a remote up into the air, presses a button and the garage door opens. He drives us in and parks the car.

'Home sweet home,' he says quietly.

I can't believe it. I live in a mansion.

6

I am shell shocked. The house is far bigger than I imagined. We must have money and lots of it. Tom gets out of the car and comes around to my side to help me out. Holding the door open for me, he takes my hand and gently pulls me out of the car. I'm glad of the help. Getting in was fine but getting out I feel my ribs pressing against my lungs causing me to wince in pain.

'Come on then, let's get you inside and settled,' Tom says. He has his kind smile painted on his face.

He gets my bag from the boot and guides me to a side door leading from the garage to the house. Holding the door open for me, I enter. It leads to a large open plan kitchen-diner. Beautifully designed, pastel earth-stone kitchen units surround all kinds of modern kitchen appliances. Many of them I don't recognise and wouldn't have a clue how to operate. The room is separated by a long breakfast bar with two stools tucked in underneath.

My eyes move to the other end of the kitchen where a six-seated oak dining table is laid out with mats and plates. Double French windows show off a field of trees and pot plants and wildflowers. Our garden, I presume. Well-kept and maintained, the garden has a terrace outside the French windows with dining table and chairs for al-fresco eating.

This is just the start. I am in awe of what we have already and don't feel ready to explore any further. I sit at the dining table and with my chin resting on my hands I let my eyes take in my surroundings.

'Are you OK?' Tom asks. 'It's a lot to take in, huh?'

'Yes.' I don't know what else to say, I am stunned.

Tom takes the seat next to me and leans in towards me. He doesn't touch me; he's learnt his lesson there. 'We've done very well for ourselves, Zoe. You chose this kitchen, in fact, you designed the whole house. But your pride and joy is your garden.'

I say nothing. I hate gardening, don't I? I can't believe I have green fingers. I thought I hated weeding and digging and planting. I wouldn't have the first idea about plants and what sunlight they need and how to grow them. But the garden is staring me in the face. If this is my pride and joy, I must enjoy gardening and I must be good at it.

Tom taps his hands on the tabletop and gets up. 'Right, love you must be starving. I'll make us some lunch.'

'Can I make it, please?' I ask. If I stand any chance of re-building my memory, I need to start living. The first place to start is in the kitchen. I need to figure out where everything is kept. 'I want to, and feel I need to. I want us to get back to normal, whatever that may be.'

Tom laughs, 'You never cook love. You do the gardening and I cook. That's the way it works between us.' He sees my disappointed face and says, 'but if you really want to, I'll help you.'

'Thanks,' I reply. 'May I ask one favour, please?'

'Sure! Anything,' he says.

'Please can you stop calling me love? In fact, please don't call me any name other than Zoe. I'm just getting my head around the name Zoe, and it's confusing to be called anything else.' Actually, I just hate being called nicknames.

Tom nods. 'OK, no worries, I understand.'

We make our way from the dining table to the kitchen. I start looking around and opening cupboards, but I have no idea where anything is. Spotting the bread bin, I slide the door of it open and take out a loaf of whole meal bread. I slide a drawer open, hoping it's the cutlery drawer. Nope, it's where the tea towels are kept. The next drawer I open contains kitchen foil and film. On the third attempt, I find the cutlery drawer and take out a knife.

The fridge is easy to spot. It's like a greengrocer's inside. There's a whole world of different vegetables, some of which I've never seen before. I take out tomatoes, lettuce and cucumber. 'Is a ham sandwich OK for you?'

'That'd be lovely. Do you want me to slice the bread?' Tom says.

'Please, that would be great.'

We work together. Tom slices the bread and I butter it. It feels good to be doing something normal. Even though it's just making a sandwich, I feel as though I'm doing something worthwhile. I open the packet of wafer-thin ham and can't resist. I never can. I take a slice and pop it in my mouth and it tastes divine.

I hear a clatter and Tom has dropped the knife on the floor. He's staring at me with his mouth wide open and my chewing slows. What on earth have I done?

Tom finally engages his brain with his mouth and says, 'Love, sorry I mean Zoe, you don't eat meat.'

What? I love meat. I love all kinds of meat. I used to joke that I was a meat-etarian. Didn't I? I swallow.

'I ... really? A vegetarian? I could have sworn ...'

'You haven't eaten meat for fifteen years, Zoe,' he explains. 'Your body's not used to it.'

Thirty seconds later, my body rejects it and I throw-up in the kitchen sink. Tom holds back my hair and rubs my back.

It may be a small issue and I'm sure I'm going to come across bigger hurdles, but this really upsets me. This new body I have is telling me what I can and can't do. My mind tells me I love meat and my body screams differently.

I pour a glass of water and sip. I feel better although throwing up has made my hunger more intense. Tom tells me to go and take a seat at the table; he'll finish off the sandwiches and bring them over. I do as I'm told.

'Why did I turn vegetarian Tom?' I ask.

'You just never really liked meat. You used to eat a bit of chicken, but it always disagreed with you. So, you just stopped eating it.' He replied.

He brings over a ham sandwich for himself and an egg salad sandwich for me. I hate eggs and look at his sandwich, salivating. I glance back at mine in my hands and brave a bite. It actually tastes delicious. Salty egg on top of sweet crisp lettuce with a juicy tomato sliced on top, all crammed into two wedges of whole meal bread. My taste buds have changed too.

We finish our lunch and I need to freshen up. 'I'd like to take a shower, if you don't mind?'

'You don't have to ask my permission! I'll show you where the bedroom is. There's an en-suite attached so you can freshen up in there. There are freshly washed clothes in the wardrobe as well, so you can take your pick,' he says.

I don't have to ask his permission. But I feel as though I do. I'm in a strange house with a man I met two weeks ago. I'm a guest in my own home.

We leave the kitchen and Tom leads me to a grand spiralled staircase in the main hall. Neatly hung on the walls above the oak banister are ornately framed photos. A stair-case gallery of Tom and the face that stared back at me in the hospital mirror. As we climb the steps, I take in the pictures of holidays, lazy summer afternoons and romantic sunsets. All featuring both Tom and me. I truly am beautiful. I'm confident, perhaps some would say arrogant but then who wouldn't be at least slightly arrogant when they are the epitome of perfect. Right at the top of the staircase, in its pride of place is a large, canvas print of us kissing on our wedding day.

Entering the bedroom, I am faced instantly with a king sized four-poster-bed. Purple satin sheets cover it with sumptuous matching cushions neatly laid along one end. The carpet is cream and shagged. Two doors lead off either side of the bedroom. Tom tells me the bathroom is through the one on my right and the walk-in wardrobe is through the one on my left.

'I'll leave you alone, to get used to where everything is. But, if you need anything, call me on this phone by the bed. Just press and hold number one and I'll be straight up,' Tom tells me.

We have a walk-in wardrobe and an intercom service?

I open the door to the wardrobe. It's practically another room. I am faced with rungs and rungs of clothes. One rung is full of Tom's clothes and three are of mine. There's a shoe rack that reaches the ceiling. There must be over a hundred pairs of shoes, all laid out meticulously in pairs. About fifty of them are all different kinds of his and hers trainers. The rest are formal male shoes and high heels. I see strappy sandals, platforms, peep toes, kittens and stilettos. My eyes widen at the height of some of these. How on earth does someone balance on those? I don't think I've worn heels since I was eighteen. But the evidence here tells me I must have.

A floor length mirror stands at the end of the wardrobe. I see my full reflection for the first time in the flesh. I have become adjusted to my face and all its features and I've just seen my body in those photos, but I haven't looked directly at it. I am tiny. Wearing the jeans and fitted T-shirt from the hospital, I can see that my hips, waist and shoulders are in perfect proportion. I have an hour-glass figure. I turn around and look over my shoulder at my back. My bum is perfectly round and pert.

I'm facing the rungs of my clothes. There are only two pairs of jeans I can see. The rest of the items are skirts, dresses, skimpy tops, long flowing trousers, cardigans and suits. A shelving unit is to the side of the rungs, again going all the way up to the ceiling. The top shelves are packed with what look like gym kits. T-shirts, tracksuits, leggings, lycra tops, crop tops, wristbands and weight training gloves. The bottom shelves are full of underwear. A shelf dedicated to boxer shorts, another for socks, one for bras and another for knickers.

Turning back round to face the mirror, I look again at my reflection and now understand how much I work to keep my body in this shape. I must be an exercise addict.

I take some underwear, a pair of jeans and a tracksuit top and head for the bathroom.

The bathroom is like my own spa. There is a square bath set in the middle of the room with steps leading up to it on all sides. A shower big enough for four people stands along the far wall. There is a toilet, two sinks and a bidet along the wall to one side and the other wall supports a worktop stretching along the length of it.

A hair dryer, hair straighteners and shaver rest on one end of the worktop, plugged into the wall next to a mirror that extends along the length of it. There is a whole pharmacy of make-up and health care treatments along with bottles of different shampoos, conditioners, moisturisers, toners and cleansers all laid out with labels facing outwards.

I take a bottle of shampoo and some shower gel and head for the shower. Standing in the vast shower space, I let the water beat down on my shoulders with a whirring groan. I feel every drop of water hit my skin like tiny pin pricks. It is amazing. My skin is massaged and soothed with every drop.

Laying a towel along the floor, I step out of the shower and dry myself. I put on the underwear and jeans and pull the tracksuit top over my head. Switching on the hairdryer, I embrace the warm air breathing over my hair and face. I pick up one of the three hairbrushes on offer and smooth out the strands of hair.

After turning off the dryer, I hear that the phone by the bedside is buzzing. I walk over to it, sit on the bed and pick it up.

'Hello?' I say.

'Just checking you're OK and you've found everything you need,' Tom says.

'Yes, thank you,' I reply. 'I'll come down in a minute.'

'No worries take your time. I'll be in the kitchen.' He hangs up.

This is like a dream. We are so rich. How did we get the money for a place like this? The memories I have of Luke and my past life suddenly seem like the reality again and this seems like the illusion. Sitting on the bed, I'm so confused. Why don't I remember any of this? This is like a hotel. It's exciting to see where everything is kept but it's not home.

I need to find out more about my life. I need to ask Tom questions. What type of person am I? I must love my body and work hard to keep it that way. All these types of clothes and shoes, the lotions and potions in the bathroom, everything is pointing to a vain woman. That's not who I want to be and it's not who I am, is it?

It's time to go and get some answers. I stand in the doorway of the bedroom and look right then left. Which way did we come? I have no idea which direction the stairs are in. This house is like a maze. There's a corridor in each direction, so I take the right. I chose correctly and head down the stairs.

The kitchen door is open, so I walk through and see Tom sat at the breakfast bar, reading a paper.

'Hey,' I say.

'Oh, hi,' Tom replies. He quickly puts the newspaper in the bin. 'You alright? Feel better after your shower?'

He looks shifty. He's hiding something from me. What's in the newspaper he doesn't want me to see?

'Yes, thanks,' I reply. 'Is there any interesting news in the paper?'

He twitches. 'No, not really, just the same old crap.'

I walk over to the bin to retrieve the paper. I'm curious. He's hiding something. He may be trying to protect me, but I need to know what the papers are saying.

'No, don't,' he begs. My eyes widen and I ignore his pleas. I open the bin and flip the paper, so the front page is staring me in the face.

The headline plastered in big black letters says: *COMA GIRL'S 'SECRET' LIFE.*

7

Stretching out the paper across the kitchen table, I sit down and start to read the article.

COMA GIRL'S 'SECRET' LIFE

Zoe Young, 30, of Taunton, was discharged from hospital today after a three-week stay. Insiders tell us that Mrs Young has been undergoing psychiatric help after emerging from a coma with amnesia. She remembers nothing of her life with her husband, Tom, but believes she has led a completely different life from the one she has woken up to.

A head-on collision, which occurred on July 22, resulted in Mrs Young's two-day coma. It is reported the driver of the other car …

Tom snatches the paper from me. 'I think you've read enough for now. I don't want you getting upset about what the papers are saying about you. I just want you to recover.'

'But I need to know,' I say. 'I need answers. I have so many questions buzzing around my head.'

'Then ask me,' he says as he rips up the paper and throws it into the bin. He takes the bin bag and its contents out to the garden ready for the bin men to collect.

On his return to the kitchen, I frown at him and say, 'I can't believe you did that. I need to know what happened that day. I need to know our past before the accident, and I need to know more about the actual car crash.'

I feel so angry. This man has no right to control me. How dare he tell me what I can and can't read?

'You will find out, in good time,' he says. 'Like you said you have so many questions going through your head. Please let me answer them one at a time.'

I can think of a few to start with. 'OK, first question, who am I? I now know I don't eat meat. What else do I need to know? What do I do for a living? Why are we so rich? What are my hobbies, other than exercise and gardening? What are my beliefs, my religion, am I Christian …?'

'That's more than one question Zoe, let me stop you there. We've got a lot of ground to cover. I'm going to make us a cup of coffee, and then I'll try and answer them as best I can.'

He brings two cups of coffee over to the kitchen table, sits down and starts talking. He starts by telling me how we met.

We met four years ago at our gym. As a fitness instructor, I'd just finished taking an aerobics lesson and was sorting out the takings, when he came over to me asking for help with his machine. He was using a neck, shoulder and chest machine when it got jammed. Having worked for the gym for two years, I knew how to unjam it as it normally happened at least once a week. Half-a-minute later and the machine was unjammed, Tom was ready to go back to his workout and we had our first date arranged.

Tom is a body builder, and a highly successful one. He has won many competitions and he tells me he has a shelf of trophies in the living room. He doesn't boast about it, but I can tell he's incredibly proud of his achievements. He works at the same gym as I do and has done for the last two years but for the social aspect rather than the income.

I listen intently to his stories and quietly sip my coffee. This is exactly what I need to be doing. I need to hear about our lives together, and about me. Nothing seems to be jogging my memory at the moment, but it's early days, I guess.

He continues to tell me about my passion for music. As well as being fit and sporty, I am a talented musician. I sing apparently and play the piano. My favourite piece of classical music is Rachmaninoff's *Rhapsody on a Theme of Paganini.* I've performed at many local gigs and concerts but don't wish to pursue it as a career. Tom tells me it's my hobby and that's how I'd like it to stay.

Looking down at my fingers, I can tell they were made for playing the piano. I can't believe I can sing though. Luke used to tell me to shut up if I started singing, he'd say I sounded like a drowning cat. Stop thinking of Luke and listen to what Tom is saying to me, I tell myself.

Apparently, I am an agnostic. I have no beliefs but am open to the idea of religion. I thought I was a Christian, brought up in the Christian faith. Well, beliefs can change, can't they? And, if Tom's telling me I'm agnostic, then he shouldn't be surprised if I start to believe in God.

I ask Tom about my family and why no-one came to visit me in hospital apart from him. He tells me I am an only child and my parents are both dead. I knew they were dead, but I ask him how they died. My father died when I was twenty-seven, a year after I met Tom. He finally passed away after a five-year battle with prostate cancer. My mother died the following year, unexpectedly in a car accident. Tom explains that that was why he was so concerned about me after my accident. He smiles and tells me, even though I don't remember him, at least I am alive and he has me back in his life.

My parents were rich. Tom explains that this is why we have such a wonderful house and are so lucky to have money. After my mum passed away, I inherited their money. Although Tom tells me when I received the money, I didn't know what to do with it. I just spent the next week sobbing. I didn't want their money, I wanted them.

The last three years must have been very tough then. No wonder Tom was so keen to look after me in hospital, he's looked after me since we met. I seem very dependent on him.

That must be why he's so quick to protect me. Like with the newspaper article.

This conversation has been a massive help. Tom has filled in some gaps, but there are many more to fill.

The rest of the afternoon and evening is spent touring the mansion then relaxing in front of the TV in the living room. The TV is an eighty-five-inch plasma and dominates the room. I find out that Tom is a bit of a softy. He loves soap operas. He tells me we watch all of them together, but I don't remember. I have no idea about the plots, or who all the characters are, but I watch them with him, pretending to know what's going on.

We eat dinner in front of the TV and watch it into the late hours of the evening. Then a thought dawns on me. Where am I going to sleep? I'm not ready to share a bed with Tom. That's going a little too far on my first night here. I don't want to offend him, but I can't bear the thought of him snuggling up next to me.

'Tom,' I say. 'Where am I sleeping tonight? Only…' I can't find the words. I really don't want to upset him.

'Don't worry,' he says, giving me that kind smile. 'I'll be in the spare room tonight so you can have our bed to yourself. I already thought of that. I think it'd be a little uncomfortable if we were to, um...'

'Thank you,' I smile back at him. 'That's very considerate of you and I really appreciate it. I'm sure it won't be for long, but I need to adjust, you know?'

'I know,' he says. 'I meant what I said at the hospital, I'll look after you, and I'll wait for you. However long it takes.'

Tom's love for me is abundantly clear. Zoe's a lucky girl to be loved so much by one man. I'm a lucky girl. I'm sure with Tom's love he'll bring my memories back. He'll help me. As he said - however long it takes.

*

I've been home for a week now. Gradually, I'm starting to settle into a routine. I've not started work yet. Tom told me I wouldn't have to go back to work for at least another month. Work has been very understanding. They sent me a lovely get-well card and flowers. The flowers have since died, but the card is still on the mantelpiece.

There are only three other cards on it. One is from a lady called Barbara and her husband Jim, our neighbours, Tom told me. Another card is from Tom's parents, Philip and Susan, whom I've yet to meet. I dread seeing them as it will be more people who love me, that I don't recognise. Thankfully they live in London, so we don't see them that often. The last card is from Tom's brother, Mark. He also lives in London, so again, not someone I have to meet in a hurry.

It's quite sad to think I didn't get many cards. Am I not liked by many people? Don't I have any friends? I must have at least one friend, or a best friend. I think of Gemma and how she would spoil me rotten every birthday.

Gemma would always put my present in a box three times as big and fill it with sweets before wrapping. It became a ritual. Every birthday, I would know I'd have a week's supply of sweets and a thoughtful present from my best friend. She'd always make me a birthday cake as well. Every year, without fail, she'd pretend that she forgot my cake. Then she'd not-so-secretly 'light' one, with Luke's help, and excitedly bring it in to me belting out *Happy Birthday to you.*

I miss Gemma. But she's not real, just as my memories of Luke and my parents aren't real. This is my life and I have to remember that.

A pang of guilt builds up inside me. I ripped Tom's card up whilst I was in hospital. That card should be standing proud on the mantelpiece as well. I treated Tom so badly. I guess it's understandable after what I went through, but I can see he's a wonderful man now that I've gotten to know him.

Tom took time off work too so that he could look after me. He's due to go back to work next week. But since having the time off, he's done nothing but spoil me.

He's taken me to our local pub in our village and shown me where I stand to sing. The pub landlord was lovely; he made me feel completely at ease and not out of place at all. Tom's driven me around Taunton, some of which I actually recognised. I seem to have many memories of Taunton, none of which feature Tom. That was the first bit of recognition I've had since returning home. Although confusing, it felt good. He showed me the gym where I work. We didn't go inside, but I observed from the comfort of our car.

This afternoon, Tom is taking me to Monkton Elm garden centre. Apparently, I used to love walking around the centre, looking at plants and buying items for our garden. As well as at the gym, it's where I felt at home. Tom's hoping I get some of the feelings back that I used to get when I'd go there.

I look at my watch. Time is getting on so I get myself ready for our trip. I actually feel quite excited about going somewhere that means something to me. Perhaps, it will trigger some real memories of mine.

Tom and I set off in the car. It's a ten-minute drive to the garden centre. I watch the fields rush past the passenger window of the Mazda and I feel good. I feel as though I'm making progress. I know, before the accident, I would have felt excited about going to the garden centre. So, it's a big relief to feel excited today. I feel the most normal I have in weeks.

We slow to a junction. I know this junction. Suddenly a feeling of dread pours over me and I start to shake. This is it, this is where it happened. We're at the *Camel Hump*.

8

I close my eyes and images flash in my mind. Everything is in a slow-moving grey haze.

I'm driving. I don't know what car I'm in, but I'm driving. Tears are streaming down my face, but I don't know why. My heart is pounding and beating rapidly. My stomach is knotted up, churning and twirling around and around. I hear the most piercing noise of screeching brakes and look to the right. A car is hurtling towards my door. Panic floods through me, I scream and then I am consumed by blackness.

I gasp for air and my eyes shoot open.

'Oh shit,' Tom says. 'I didn't think. Are you alright?'

I'm panting and shaking all over. Do I look alright? No, I'm not. I've just regained my first memory of the accident, and it wasn't pleasant.

'Not really. This is where it happened. I just saw … well, I remember … A car hit me. They hit me!'

I can't control my emotions. It really happened. It happened here. Tom steps on the gas and gets me away from the scene of the crash. He pulls into the garden centre car park and parks the car. He looks over to me once the engine is turned off.

'Oh, Zoe,' he says. 'I shouldn't have driven that way. I just didn't think.'

He shakes his head and looks mortified at his actions. It's not his fault though. Perhaps he didn't think, but I'm the one who's been going on and on about getting back to normality. Doing my normal thing and getting my normal life back on track.

My breathing is slowing, but I can't get the images out of my head. The sound of the screeching brakes and the skidding of the other car before it plunged bonnet-first into my door.

'It's not your fault,' is all I can manage.

We sit in the car in silence. Tom stares out of his window. I have a feeling he's crying softly. I have my head in my hands. I'm trying to rub away the horrible memories from my mind. It's stupid. All I've wanted since leaving the hospital is to regain some of my lost memories. As soon as I remember something, I want rid of it. It's just typical it's the worst memory that comes back first. I guess this is what normally happens. The most recent event, before memory loss, is the worst event. It's what caused the amnesia. As it's the most recent event, it's what's fresh in the mind, so I'm guessing it comes to the surface first.

I turn to look at Tom. He has his face buried in his right arm. His arm's resting on the edge of the car window. I hear the odd sniff.

'Tom,' I say. 'Please don't worry. I need to remember things. I just wish that wasn't the first thing I remembered. But, it's a good sign, hey? Other memories should start to surface now, shouldn't they?'

He raises his head from his arm, his eyes red and cloudy. 'I am sorry,' he says.

'You've no reason to be. I should be thanking you really. OK it's not the best thing to remember, but it shows I'm capable of remembering things. Tom, I could recover.'

Tom smiles, thank goodness for that. He needs to be strong.

'I feel so helpless, Zoe,' Tom says. 'I normally have the words or know what to do to make things better for you. But I have no idea what to do to help you.'

Tom is used to being the strong one. I get it. He has helped me through so much in the last few years, especially after both my parents died. But he doesn't know how to help me now. All he needs to do is to be himself and keep doing what he's doing.

'You're doing fine, Tom,' I smile at him through tear-stained eyes. 'You're helping me more than you know. Just be patient, I will get there. I feel positive after regaining my first memory.'

Tom smiles back at me. 'You really are remarkable. I love you so much. I hope you start to remember more every day.'

I hope so too. I hope I remember enough of my previous life to start saying *I love you* back to Tom. I hope I remember enough about me, to start enjoying exercise and gardening. I hope one day I forget how lovely meat tastes. I hope one day I forget about Luke, Gemma, mum and dad. But I don't believe that will ever happen.

*

Over the next few days, the nightmares begin.

Last night was the worst. I dreamt I was torn in two. All the nightmares centre on the car accident, the location is always the Camel Hump and I'm always driving. Normally, I replay the memories of the accident in my mind, but last night was different.

Driving up to the junction, I had the radio blaring as my eyes streamed with tears. This part was normal, my nightmares always start this way. I turned up the music and then things in the nightmare started to change.

My mum was sat in the passenger seat and dad, Luke and Gemma were all sat in the back. They were all singing loudly to the music, laughing and enjoying themselves. I was miserable. It was like it was the worst day of my life and I was going to lose them all. They didn't know this, but I knew in my heart, this was the last time I would see them all together, with me.

Pulling out of the junction, Gemma shrieked, 'Aisha, stop!'

I slammed my foot on the brakes and the car spun round and round. It spun faster and faster. The car was like a spinning top, in the middle of the road, just spinning on the spot.

As it gradually slowed down, my eyes began to focus again. Everyone had vanished. The car had turned into a Mazda identical to Tom's and I had the roof down. On the passenger seat was a pink baby's dummy. I looked down at my body and from head down to foot I'd been torn in half. I only had the left side of my body remaining.

I screamed as loud and for as long as I could, until I heard Tom's calming voice in my ear, telling me it was just a nightmare, and felt his hand rubbing my forehead.

Each nightmare I have seems to have a little more detail in it. But I don't know what's true anymore. I don't know which are memories and which ones are dreams.

Tonight, my nightmare is like last night's.

The dream starts the same as always. I drive up to the junction, music blaring, tears rolling down my cheeks. Mum, dad, Luke and Gemma are all in the car with me, singing along to the music. When Gemma shrieks, '*Aisha, stop,*' I look at her in the rear-view mirror and slam my foot on the accelerator instead of the brake. The car slams into another car and spins round and round, faster and faster. Again, like a spinning top.

Once the car has slowed down again, my eyes come into focus. Everyone has vanished, I am torn in half, just as I was in last night's dream, but Tom is sat on the passenger side of the car this time. In his arms he holds a baby.

I wake up, sweating and shaking as normal. Tom is gently rubbing his thumb along my forehead, calming me down with his soothing words. I don't understand what these nightmares mean. Why are there references to babies in them? Perhaps it means new life. I have always been fascinated with dreams and their meanings. The reference to babies could mean a new life for me. What if there's a reason why my life before the accident has been wiped from my mind. Maybe I'm supposed to build a new life for myself, rather than re-build my old one.

Today is the start of my life. My new life with Tom and my new life as Zoe. I'm not going to focus on trying to remember my old life. I want to build new memories now.

*

Tom has started back at work today. I haven't got anything to do other than a food shop. He left the house at five-thirty this morning as he's working the early shift at the gym. He should be home by one-thirty this afternoon. It's now nine-thirty, so I need to get ready to go shopping.

This will be the first time I've left the house on my own. I feel I'm ready to do this, but it still seems like such a big task ahead of me. I just need to go to the supermarket to get a few things, but because I'll be on my own, it is a bit daunting. I must think of it as a massive achievement.

We're going out for the afternoon after Tom's finished work. We're going to go to Cheddar Gorge and down into the caves. It's a treat to congratulate me for going out of the house alone. Tom though it would motivate me to start doing things myself. I don't know if I've ever been to the gorge before. I don't believe I have but I don't really care if I've been there before or not.

I'm very excited. Not to go down in the caves, or to see the gorge, but to start living again. Tom's shown me around Taunton, taken me shopping in the town and shown me our favourite haunts. But I want to explore. I want to explore outside of Taunton now. I want to see places I never knew existed. Tom will be with me when we go to the gorge, so every memory I make will have him in them.

It's a strange thing. I don't remember Tom or anything to do with our life before the accident, but I still recognise places not associated with Tom. It seems to be the important memories I have lost. I know of Cheddar Gorge, I can't say I've been there, but I know it. I also remember roads. I remember routes and shortcuts. There are so many trivial things I do remember, but nothing about Tom. So, this is why it's so important to start building new memories.

I have my shower, get dressed and grab my purse. I'm not well enough to drive yet so I must get the bus. I had to hand in my driver's licence until I get a clean bill of health from the doctor. The next bus leaves in ten minutes.

I lock the front door and run. If I don't catch this bus, there won't be another one for an hour. This is one of the disadvantages of living in the country. All my bruising has healed now, so I'm able to run freely and I realise how fast I am.

Running is an ease. I'm not panting, puffing or gasping. I'm happily sprinting along, inhaling and exhaling gently and feeling the cool breeze in my hair. I reach the bus stop, just as the bus pulls up. I dig into my pocket to retrieve my inhaler. It's an automatic response as I'm a little out of breath after my mile-long dash. I realise I don't need it. I could have sworn I was asthmatic. I shake my head. Little things like this keep popping into my mind, but I must push them to the back and focus on the reality.

There are a number of seats available on the bus, so I pay the driver and sit down. I look around at the other passengers. I feel self-conscious. What if they recognise me, but I don't know who they are? Tom told me last night, if anyone talks to me as if they know me, I need to tell them: *If you know me, then you'll know I'm recovering from a head injury.*

Unfortunately, I don't remember you. Now, if you'll excuse me, I must get going. I know it sounds harsh, but I can't be doing with strangers talking to me, and asking me how I am. I just want to get on with my new life.

No-one sits next to me, thankfully. There is an elderly lady sat on the seat in front of me and a young couple sit the other side of the aisle from me. They are holding hands and giggling into each other's ears. They are obviously in love. I miss that.

The bus pulls up outside the supermarket. I take a deep breath and walk off the bus. I am standing in front of a large white and green building with people bustling around me, fighting with shopping trolleys and bags.

I can get this done in thirty minutes if I put my mind to it. I grab a small shopping trolley and head down the aisles. I grab everything on my list and make my way to the checkout.

Thirty-two pounds lighter, I carry my bags out of the supermarket. I have fifteen minutes before my bus arrives again. I stop in my tracks. Shit, I forgot batteries for my camera. I need to take photos of the gorge; I need to capture new moments. I turn around to head back into the supermarket, without any consideration for other people. I swing round, straight into the chest of a man.

'Oh, gosh, I'm so sorry.' As I say these words, I lift my head to look at the man. My jaw drops.

I am staring straight into the beautiful blue eyes of Luke. Beside him, holding his hand is a remarkably familiar brown haired, freckly, hazel-eyed girl.

Part 2

9

'Aisha, darling,' my mother called. 'Where are you? Lunch is ready.'

'Coming, mum,' I replied.

It was the school summer holidays, and I was about to turn ten. Most of my summer days were spent in the garden. I loved being outside, listening to the birds and smelling the countryside air. Even if it was raining, I'd take my mother's brolly and wander around the garden hearing and watching the drops fall around me.

My dad built me a wooden house in our biggest apple tree. Many an afternoon during the holidays, I'd take a book and sit and read in my tree house. I'd get lost in a world of fantasy and fairy tales and imagine myself as characters from my books.

I always wanted a sister. I grew up with Gemma, since the age of five, and she was like a sister to me. But she had an older sister of her own. I would watch the both of them whenever I stayed at Gemma's house. They would play together and laugh and just have fun. When I was on my own at home, I didn't have anyone to play with. So, I played alone.

My teddy bears played a big part in my games. I would take my three favourite teddies, sit them down in my tree house, and talk to them. I made up all sorts of games. Mainly I would imagine that I was a princess, waiting for my prince charming to arrive on a big white horse to rescue me from the evil witch. One of my teddies was always my fairy godmother, another the evil witch and the third was always my loyal friend.

Before my mother called me for lunch, I was playing my favourite game where my fairy godmother would grant me three wishes. Whatever I wished for would come true.

I spread a picnic blanket out on the grass lawn and sat my teddies in a semi-circle on it. In the middle of the lawn was a ring of toadstools. I absolutely loved this ring. Every year, towards the end of the summer, it would die, but the following summer it would grow back again. At least once every summer I would stand in the middle of the ring to make my three wishes.

Every time I played this game, I wished for the same three things. I'd wish my prince charming would come and sweep me off my feet and that I had a sister to play with. And I'd always wish I was pretty.

Even from an early age, I always wanted to be thin and pretty. I hated my body for as long as I could remember. I was always the chubby child at school; the kid other parents would talk about, saying *she's big for her age* or *you wouldn't think she was the same age as my daughter.*

Throughout my childhood, I'd never felt normal. I wasn't one of the pretty ones. I was never slim and sporty. I was freckly, overweight and asthmatic. All I ever wanted was to look like someone else.

*

In the supermarket, time stands still. I look at Luke, then I look at her, then I look at Luke again. My eyes dart back and forth between the two of them. This is my life, standing here, right in front of me. This is me; this is my husband. I am frozen on the spot, just staring at the two of them. I look at her again. She stares back at me with wide, frightened eyes. She is a rabbit caught in my headlights. But she can't hold my gaze and looks away. A red blush gradually appears across her cheek.

'Are you OK, miss?' Luke asks me.

Luke's face begins to grow fuzzy, the lights of the supermarket glow too brightly, my head swirls.

'No, I'm not OK,' I say. My heart thumps in my chest. You're real Luke. But, you don't recognise me. 'I'm sorry … sorry.'

My knees buckle underneath me, the shopping bags fall to the floor and as my head hits the ground, darkness rears its ugly head once again.

*

'Steady, I'm going to raise your head so that you can drink some water,' Luke says.

My eyes open slowly, everything is a blur, the room is still spinning, but I see Luke beside me, looking over me. I gasp. It was all a dream. Luke's here, I must be in hospital after the car accident. He knows who I am and he's looking after me. My heart is in my mouth and I smile at Luke, the man I love who's caring for me.

But then other things start to come into focus. I can see the lighting and metal beams stretching along the roof above me and hear the noise of children screaming, tannoy announcements and the clattering of shopping trolleys.

'You've just fainted,' Luke says. 'Do you think you can stand? There's a chair just in front of you.'

It was too good to be true; of course, it wasn't a dream. It was a nice feeling whilst it lasted. Taking my time, I clamber to my feet, my head rushes again causing blindness, but gradually the darkness clears allowing me to see the chair in front of me, so I sit down. Luke hands me a glass of water.

A female shop assistant stands by me and asks, 'Do you want me to call an ambulance? Or, do you think you'll be OK? You gave us a bit of a fright then!'

To show my gratitude, I smile at her and say, 'No, thank you, an ambulance won't be necessary. I'm just going to sit here a second, then I'll leave you in peace.'

'Oh, take your time and enjoy your water,' she says smiling at me.

Luke's kind eyes curl up at the corners as he smiles at me. Over in the corner of the supermarket foyer, close to the exit doors, *she* stands, arms folded. She looks very impatient, tapping her feet and checking her watch.

'I think we can go now Luke,' she says. 'She's in safe hands.'

She's itching to get away. You can see how awkward she feels just by looking at her scrunched up freckly face.

'Is there anyone I can call for you before I go?' Luke asks.

'No, thank you.'

He turns to face *her*. 'OK Aisha, I think she's OK, so let's make a move.'

'Yes, come on then love, time's ticking,' *She* replies whilst tapping her left wrist and throwing me a glare.

He turns back to me and says, 'Take care of yourself then and only head home when you're ready.'

They head towards the automatic exit doors and just as they exit, *she* turns to look at me over her shoulder, head low and eyes staring up at me under her furrowed brow. She slowly raises the index finger of her right hand to the middle of her forehead and throws a rather threatening point in my direction. As if to say, 'I'm watching you.'

They both leave the supermarket.

I finish off my glass of water with shaking hands, use another five minutes to gather myself, take my re-packed bags and head towards the bus stop.

As I reach the bus stop, that's when it hits me. I perch on the hard, red plastic seat inside the bus shelter and put my head in my hands. I want to get home now. But where is my home? Is it really with Tom, the man I was gradually getting to know and actually like? It never felt like my home, and it feels even less like home now. But I need to leave this supermarket, even if it means heading back there. Time ticks by so slowly whilst I'm waiting. Please come soon bus.

The bus is late. But of course it's late. Buses never run on time when you really need them to. It pulls up at the bus shelter, and I board.

The bus is busy. Taking a window seat towards the back I put my shopping on the seat next to me. I stare out of the window.

'Can I squeeze next to you, my love?' An elderly woman stands next to my seat.

Now that's just typical. She's elderly so I can't exactly say no. All I want is to sit here alone and sob quietly and unnoticeably. I glance around, and I can count at least another five seats available. But no, she wants to sit next to *me*. So, *I* have to move *my* bags, and *I* have to listen to her inane conversations all the way home no doubt.

I take a deep breath, nod and grab my bags, forcing them in-between my legs and onto my lap. I am now buried amongst my weekly shopping. I can't even hold my head in my hands now, or wipe my cheeks, or blow my nose, as I have to hold onto the bloody bags.

My nose is running. I sniff every few seconds, trying to stop it trickling down my lip. I raise my shoulder to my face and manage to wipe my nose on my jumper. Not the nicest of things to do, but necessary.

The woman next to me places her wrinkly, sun-spotted hand on my arm and says, 'I can't help noticing, but you seem a bit upset my love. Are you alright?'

Well, if she's noticed I'm a little bit upset, then I guess it would be obvious that I'm not alright, wouldn't it?

'I'm fine thank you,' I say, bluntly.

'You know, when people say they're fine, they're not. It's a very negative thing to say actually. So, I don't think you are alright.'

Bravo old lady. Well done for stating the bloody obvious. No, I'm not alright, I'm not fine but I'd be better if you shut up.

But she doesn't shut up, she continues. 'I get a feeling about you. Let me give you some advice. You can never ignore good advice, you never know when you may need it, or where it may take you.'

'Some things in life just happen.' She continues. 'There's no avoiding them and there's no stopping them. You've got to just go with it. Everyone is on a journey through life. Each person follows their own path. There are many twists and turns, missed roads and opportunities and people who just pass you by and never form part of your life path. Sometimes the path takes you somewhere you never imagined going with someone you never imagined meeting. But this is life, and we all must head down our individual paths no matter what lurks behind the next corner. We've just got to keep going.'

I turn to look at the lady through teary, blurred eyes. She must be in her mid-seventies. Her glasses are perched neatly on the end of her nose and she's watching me over their rim. She has a stern expression; that of a teacher to a pupil, but there is warmth behind her specs.

The bus pulls over and the lady says, 'Well, this is my stop, love. Keep following your path but look out for side roads. Don't let them pass you by.'

With that she was gone.

I stare out of the window as the bus pulls back out again to carry on its journey. Trees and houses and car driveways whizz past me. My eyes glaze over, not focussing on anything. Then the reflection in the window brings my eyes back to focus. There it is; the perfectly symmetrical face, the chiselled jaw and the blonde bob. I am Aisha in a stranger called Zoe's body. The bus slows. The next stop is mine.

*

Standing, staring at the front door, shopping bags scattered around my feet, I rummage in my pocket for the front door keys. Letting myself in, I take the bags into the kitchen and put them on the table. I sit down at the dining table and vacantly stare into space.

I rub my forehead. I am no longer crying but I'm in a daze. I feel so lonely again. Who can I talk to about today? Anyone I turn to will think I'm mad and send me back to rehab again for more brainwashing. I have no friends; no family and my so-called husband would be useless to talk to about this. Tom wouldn't understand, he would just try and rationalise it, probably by saying I was mistaken and that I didn't actually see what I thought I saw. But I know what I saw.

This morning, I woke up as Zoe. I wasn't entirely happy yet with being Zoe. I wasn't overly comfortable with living this forgotten life. But, for the first time since the accident, I felt excited. I was excitedly looking forward to creating new moments to treasure down in the caves, to slowly regaining some more old memories and to settling down with Tom in the here and now.

This morning, I felt the most content I'd felt in a long time. I'd started to adjust to married life with Tom and was finally looking forward to the future instead of concentrating on the past. I was hoping to start re-building a future with Tom and settle into a normal routine. Doing a normal food shop was part of this routine. Tom going back to work was part of it too. I was also looking forward to starting back at work in a few weeks' time and regaining some sort of a social life.

Now, everything has been turned on its head again. At first, I believed I was Aisha and people around me were either mad or they had their facts wrong. I thought Tom was a weirdo, claiming me as his wife and convincing the doctors I was. Then, I underwent a course of counselling in the rehab centre. Specialists focussed on separating my memories and dreams which supposedly became scrambled after the accident. The longer I stayed there, the more I accepted that I was Zoe, not Aisha.

When I moved back to my house with Tom, I started to believe this was my life, that I was Zoe. I started to understand what the doctors and specialists were trying to explain to me in rehab. I had lost my memory and replaced it with a fantasy life. This fantasy life was stopping my real memories from re-surfacing. So, I dutifully tried to block all thoughts of my made-up life with Luke and focus on my real life with Tom, as Zoe.

But, today, I stepped right into that fantasy life; the life I was made to believe wasn't real. I bumped into the husband I'd adamantly sworn existed and stood face to face with the person I'd known as my reflection for the last thirty years. I think back to when I saw her, she knew she was living my life, just as I knew I was living hers, and she was enjoying it. The threatening look she gave me as she left the supermarket, the pure hatred she cast me in her stare and the point in my direction. There was something very sinister about that finger point. Not only was it sinister but it was somewhat arrogant. She knew she had what I wanted most in the world and she was clear that she didn't want to give it back to me in a hurry.

Now, I know I am Aisha. My life and my memories are being played with. Somehow, my old life has been taken from me and I have been left to live someone else's. The lady on the bus said *keep following your path but look out for side roads. Don't let them pass you by.* This is a side road I must take. I need to change my path from living this fantasy life to getting my real life back.

I am Aisha Brown and all I want, right here, right now is my body and my life back.

*

Tom will be home in an hour and a half. I must move quickly if I want to be out of here before he gets home. I know it's cowardly of me to leave without speaking to him face-to-face, but I haven't got the energy. I need to get out of this house. It isn't helping me; I just look around and see nothing of me and everything of her. This is not my house, and the sooner I leave, the better.

I start packing. There's not much to pack as none of its mine anyway, but I do need some essentials. I pack a few items of clothing and some toiletries into a little suitcase. I still have the credit card and about thirty pounds in notes Tom gave me for the food shop so at least I know I can get by. I shove them into Zoe's purse which I still have from the hospital. I feel bad about taking Zoe's money, but then Tom thinks it's mine anyway, so he won't bat an eyelid about that. But he will be so hurt that I've left him.

Tom deserves some sort of an explanation as to why I've disappeared. I really can't cope with talking to him face-to-face, he'll only try and convince me to stay. I must write him a note. It's the coward's way out, but at least he'll know why I've gone.

Next to the phone in the bedroom is a notebook and pen. I rip a page out of the notebook and start writing. The pen takes hold and although I move the pen as I always have, the writing is different. Even my handwriting isn't my own anymore. I write:

Dear Tom,

I'm so sorry to do this but things are moving too quickly for me. I need to get away for a while and gather my thoughts. Please don't worry, I'll be fine. I just need some time on my own to think. Please don't try to contact me. I will contact you when I'm ready.

Thanks for being so kind and making me feel so welcome.

Zoe

I fold the note in half and scribble *Tom* on the front of it. I grab my bag and head downstairs. I take a last look around the house. Part of me feels a little sad to be leaving. It wasn't that long ago that I was actually starting to plan a life here with Tom. But I don't belong here. It's not right to continue this façade.

Going into the kitchen, the food shopping is still on the table waiting to be packed away. I leave it. It's not my food and it's not my kitchen. I stand the note on the kitchen worktop so it's easily visible.

I breathe in slowly and deeply, closing my eyes briefly before stepping out of the house. I lock the front door and post the keys through the letter box.

10

The world can be such a vast, lonely place when you're on your own. Everyone you see seems to be smiling and loving life. Women pushing buggies stop to hug and greet other mums, laughing and sharing parental tips. People chatting on mobile phones to their friends and loved ones blowing kisses as they hang-up. Cars zoom past with music blaring, windows down, the people inside singing crazily. Even the homeless man in the bus shelter looks content with life, greeting passers-by, making small talk, taking their money.

I've never been one to have loads of friends. Gemma was enough for me growing up. Other friends tended to just get in the way. They would come and go. Some would stay in contact after school for a few months, and then move onto their new lives. But it didn't bother me because I'd had a soul mate, one person who I could one hundred per cent rely on. Not many people could say they had found that person.

Now all I want is for someone to recognise me, anyone to shout, 'Hey Aisha, how's it going?' I don't care who it is. But as I walk down the street, no-one turns to look at me. No-one shouts out to me. No-one seems to know I even exist. They are all too busy smiling and enjoying their wonderful lives. People are bumping into people they know left, right and centre. They're too busy talking to each other, arranging coffee, organising shopping trips, talking about work, laughing and joking about the last work Christmas party to know I'm here, watching them.

'Zoe! ... Zoe?' Registering it took a while. A hand grabs my shoulder. 'Hey, you, are you alright? How's it going?'

A woman, perhaps forty years of age, dressed in gym-wear smiles at me as I turn to meet her gaze.

'Sorry... I... um... I have to go.' The woman's face drops.

'Zoe, it's me... Karen, from the gym. I'm sorry. I didn't mean to startle you.'

I just stare blankly at her for a couple of seconds, her slim figure, bright blue eyes, snub nose. 'I'm not who you think I am, sorry, you must be mistaken.' I turn on my heels, head down the street and don't look back.

*

Clouds form across the early September sky. Raindrops start to fall, light at first and then the heavens open. Dripping wet, I stop walking outside an old grey and white building. Big hanging baskets full of dying Busy Lizzies, Pansies and Geraniums surround the oak front door. The sign above the door reads, The Bear Inn.

Inside the bed and breakfast, an old man stands behind an oak counter with a stag's head hanging above his own.

'Come in, come in. This British weather is so unpredictable. Bless you, you're soaked through! What can I do for you young lady?'

Dropping my suitcase to the floor I say, 'I need a room please, if you have one? I noticed the sign outside said you have vacancies.'

The old man nods and asks for my details. I give him *my* details, the ones I was born with and am so used to.

'My name's Aisha Brown.' I give him my date of birth and address and take out my credit card from my purse.

'This card says Zoe Young. May I ask why you are trying to pay with someone else's card?'

Oh bugger. 'Oh of course, I do apologise. I'm currently going through a name change.' I know it's a lie but it's the only thing I can think of to say. 'I do apologise, I'm trying to get used to my new name, Aisha Brown, but forget sometimes that I haven't changed my name on everything. I'm sure I have my deed poll documents here somewhere.' I pretend to start rummaging in my suitcase.

Then it dawns on me that there may be a driving licence in the purse. Oh, please let there be one. Yes … thank goodness. I hand him the license with a photo of my new face and Zoe's name on it.

'That's perfect. Thank you, young lady. Just you make sure you change your name sooner rather than later; it can be confusing for folk. And I can be easily confused.' He starts cackling.

'Thank you, sir, I do appreciate it,' I say.

'Quite alright dear, and call me Arthur, no formalities at The Bear Inn. Take room number two. It's got a beautiful view of Vivary Park, with your own en-suite. I only give that room to my favourite guests.' He gives me a wink and a kind smile, so I force a smile back at him.

Room number two is cosy. A double bed spreads the length of one wall with a bedside table on one side. It's dated, but much loved. Clean, fresh-smelling and warm. There's just enough room for a small wardrobe and desk along the stretch of the other wall. A vase of daisies sits on top of the desk with pen and notepad next to it. I drop my bag down on the bed and walk over to the window to see the view of the park.

Arthur was right; the view was lovely even on a wet and miserable day like today. I could imagine in the summer months, mums and dads playing football with their children, couples spread out on blankets enjoying the sun and an ice-cream van parked up playing music, tempting the children to spend their parents' hard-earned cash.

I used to go to the park in the summer with school friends. We would sit on the swings chatting about boys and laughing about embarrassing things we'd done. Gemma would be there of course, laughing along with them all and I would normally just enjoy swinging in the sun, smiling, listening to their stories.

I look at my watch. It's almost one-thirty. Tom will be getting home soon. Have I done the right thing? I feel so sorry for him, planning our trip down the caves, getting excited about starting afresh, and then returning home to my out-of-the-blue note. Maybe I should have stayed and talked to him, but the truth is, I'm tired of thinking about his feelings, it's time to think of my own, and start re-building my life.

Now that I'm here, in this B&B, what do I do next? I sit on the edge of my bed next to my suitcase and stare ahead of me. I can't even think anymore. Closing my eyes, I lie down and curl up into a little ball protecting myself from the strange world I've found myself in and shortly drift off to sleep.

*

A metallic doorbell noise jolts me awake. I can't have been asleep for long, maybe twenty minutes. Ding dong …

ding dong … ding dong. It's my phone. I rummage through my bag trying to feel for its vibrations, retrieve it and see that it's Tom. He's home, he's got the note and he's wondering what on earth's going on. I must answer it as it's not fair on him. At the end of the day, he doesn't know where I am, and I won't tell him, so he won't be able to come and find me.

'Hello?' I ask, knowing full well who it is.

'Zoe, thank God, where the hell are you?' He sounds worried.

'I'm staying away for a few nights. I did try to explain in my note to you. I did ask that you didn't phone me.' I knew he would call, it's just typical, doesn't he realise I need time to think?

There is silence for a couple of seconds. 'Well of course I'm going to phone you. I don't get it, you were settling in, we were doing well. We were going to look to the future. We're supposed to be on our way to Cheddar right now. What's changed?'

'Nothing's changed Tom,' I say. 'I'm still the confused girl you brought home with you from rehab and staying with you doesn't seem to be improving things at the moment, I need time alone to sort things out in my head, and in my own time. I'm sorry. It's not you, it's …'

'Give me some credit Zoe, please. Spare me the *it's not you it's me speech* I think I'm worth a little more than that. I just … I … um … look, I really need to talk to you.'

I sigh. 'That's all we've done since I've been with you is talk. Talking is getting us nowhere. I'm done talking about the life I don't remember. I need to get some clarity. I can't be the person you want me to be Tom, at least not yet. I can't promise you anything but give me time and who knows.'

Tom mutters something under his breath but I can't quite make it out. 'I just don't get it Zoe. Something must have happened in the space of time between me leaving for work and you getting home with the shopping.'

Do I tell him? Do I tell him that I bumped into my husband, the husband that isn't him? That I saw the husband who I supposedly dreamed about and that doesn't exist? 'I bumped into someone today, someone from my past, my past as Aisha.'

Tom scoffs, 'We've been through this a hundred times now. Aisha doesn't exist. I need you to move on. I've been patient, but patience wears thin after a while. You are Zoe and you're married to *me*.'

There's nothing for me to say. I can understand him getting annoyed, and he's right, he has been patient with me. But I'm not Zoe and I'm certainly not married to him. Instead of responding, I just start to sob.

'Look, I'm sorry I lost it for a second there, please don't cry. Please, just come home. There's something you really need to know, and I don't want to have to tell you on the phone.'

'I'm done talking Tom. It doesn't help. Please don't call me again. I will call you when *I* am ready to hear what you need to tell me. Right now, I don't think there's any more room in my head for anything else.' I hang up.

*

It's two-thirty. There's no point in falling back to sleep again, it's hard enough to sleep now, let alone when I've slept through the day. So, I decide to start writing things down.

Sitting at the desk, I open the pad of paper, draw a line down the centre of the page and write *date* in the left-hand column and *memory* on the right. Starting with my earliest memory, I list everything I can remember about my life.

My earliest memory was when I was three and I first slept in a proper bed. I remember the feeling of the big, cushiony space all around me. My feet didn't touch the end of the bed and I felt so grown up. I continue jotting down memories until I can't remember anything else.

The last memory I write down is visiting Mrs Wyatt's house.

It's taken me three hours to write everything down, but I feel better for it. There is my life, on paper. Every memory has its place. I re-read everything I've written and think how could I possibly have made this entire life up? Unless I have very vibrant dreams, and slept for most of my life, it would be impossible.

Almost a third of these memories feature Luke. I can't believe I saw him. It was awful seeing him, wanting to hold him and kiss him but knowing he didn't know who I was. And, he was with *her,* shopping, in a supermarket, in the morning.

He should have been in school at that time. But he wasn't. Perhaps he's been looking after her and taken some time off. Or perhaps I went shopping earlier than I thought. I look in my wallet for the supermarket receipt to see the time, dropping a small piece of card onto the floor. Holding the receipt up, I can see it clearly states 11.47. She's got him looking after her. But she looked fine when I saw her, not injured or confused like me. She was happy.

On my shoe was the card that fell out. Bending down, I picked it up. It was a gym business card with Zoe's contact details on, and down the bottom of it read *zoe.young@ukintermail.com.*

Time to find out a little more about the life of Zoe Young, the life that I now seem to be living and find out who the hell is now living mine.

11

'Hi Arthur, do you know where the nearest internet café is please?'

He'd been quietly reading a novel at the reception desk, when I sprung on him. 'Crikey dear, you made me jump then. Miss Marple was just about to walk into the study to examine the body and in you burst. Not good for the old nerves!'

'Oh sorry! I didn't mean to make you jump. I'm just in a bit of a hurry that's all.'

'Don't you worry about it. Good for the old ticker, shows it's still working getting the pulse racing like that. Now then, internet café … Well, don't go rambling out and about when my missus has a laptop that I'm sure you can borrow. We've got all mod-cons here you know, even got Wi-Fi! Give me five minutes and I'll bring it to your room.'

Fantastic! I didn't really want to be going out anyways, but now I've got this email address, I didn't want to waste any time. 'Thank you, Arthur that would be truly kind, of you.'

Arthur scuttles to the bottom of the stairs behind his desk and shouts, 'Mildred! Mildred! We got one for the laptop!' He turns to face me again and says, 'Off you go then dear, back to your room, I'll see you in five.'

I head off back to room two and sure enough, five minutes after closing the door behind me there's a knock on the door. I take the lap-top from Arthur, thank him again and start setting it up on the desk.

Ukintermail is easy to find on Google. I click on the sign-in button and it asks me for my email address and password. I have no idea what the password is, so enter the email address and click on forgotten password. A security question pops up: *What's your favourite piece of music?* I think back to what Tom said it was. *Rhapsody on a Theme of Paganini* that was it! So, I type it in.

Bingo! Access into Zoe's email has been granted. I change the password to *Luke79,* easy for me to remember and change my security question.

You have 2 new messages. There's only two in a month and a half? There are several emails received since the accident which have been read. So, she's still logging on as Zoe. She is going through the same thing as me. I knew it. So why did she look so happy when I saw her? I scroll down the list. Most of them are junk messages. But a few of the read emails are from Facebook, saying there are pending notifications.

I click on *My Account* and change the security question to: *What was the name of your first pet?* The answer I type is *I never had a pet.* Hopefully, she won't be able to access her email again. Is that illegal? Have I turned into a hacker? No, no I haven't. I'm supposedly Zoe Young so, if I must use everything else of hers, I may as well use her email.

Time to start investigating, I think. The two new emails are also pending notifications. I click on the first unread email and get directed to a Facebook link asking me to enter my email address and password. On the Facebook website I click on forgotten password and enter *zoe.young@ukintermail.com* in the email box, then request my password to be emailed to me.

Logging back into my email, I receive a new message from Facebook with a code to input on the networking site. I type it in and bingo, password is reset. I use *Luke79* again to make things simple.

The face I have started to know as my reflection stares back at me on the profile page. It's a nice picture of Zoe sitting in a beer garden at a wooden picnic table. The sun is shining, but although she is smiling, something seems to be wrong about her expression. I can't quite place what, only that there is an element of sadness behind her eyes.

Zoe has fifteen *friends*. That's an unusually low amount but perhaps she hasn't been on the site for very long. I scroll down the page through her timeline, and see she joined the site three years ago. Three years and she only has fifteen *friends*? My brow furrows as I contemplate the idea of only having a few friends, knowing full well that most friends on Facebook are merely acquaintances.

My old Facebook account used to have about a-hundred-and-fifty *friends*. Not that I ever spoke to all of them. They were people I'd befriended along the way, through previous schools, jobs, clubs. Mostly acquaintances, people I would occasionally wonder about but never pick up the phone to call.

I think of Gemma. She is the only friend who has really stuck by me throughout my life. But I have other friends too. I call them my five-fingered-friends. I don't need to see them or contact them regularly to know that they are there. If ever I need them, or they need me, we'll always be at the end of the phone. Well, that's what I used to say and think, before I woke up in hospital with a new husband by my bed and a new life to lead. They wouldn't be at the end of the phone for me now; they wouldn't know who I was.

Zoe has posted that she is married to Tom Young. Tom is one of her *friends*. In fact, he's the only male friend. Her last post was dated two days ago.

Hmmm contemplating a new start, a new direction, a new life.

She wants a new start, a new direction and a new life? Oh really? My life is it? I can feel my blood start to boil. How dare she contemplate living my life, she should want her old life back as much as I want mine.

Images flash before me of Luke coming home from work, kissing *her*, asking *her* how her day was, cooking tea for the both of them. I can see both of them living a happy oblivious lie of a life. Why would she want my life? Surely, she was happy in her own. From what I've seen of her life, she had it made. She had a great job, a loving husband, a fantastic figure and a mansion to live her life in. Why she wouldn't want that back is beyond me. I like the simpler things in life, a cosy roof over my head which is a place I can call home, a loving relationship and close friends and family nearby. We lead completely different lives, I can't imagine her enjoying living mine, just like I don't and can't enjoy living hers.

There are a couple of other posts from the last two months. The first one says that she's lonely and needs a friend. No one liked the post or commented on it. The other says that she's loving her life and loving her husband.

If Tom were to read this, he would think it was me writing it and it would add to his confusion. I certainly do not love this life or Tom. What Tom wouldn't realise but is crystal clear to me is that she's referring to Luke, *my* Luke and it's my life that she's loving.

Scrolling back to the top of the page, I click on *About* to find out a little more about Zoe Young. It reads that she went to a local school, works now for *Tone-Up Fitness Group* and is married to Tom Young. My eyes almost pop out of my head when I see her birthday. She was born on the same day as me, January the first. Not just the same day, but the same year. I can't believe it and I won't believe it. We were both born on the same New Year's Day. We are exactly the same age. I feel so angry, how dare she take so much of me, even the day I was born.

Tom has his own profile, so I take a look. Thankfully he hasn't logged on for months, so he wouldn't have seen Zoe's posts. I scroll down his wall. Not much to see really, apart from online gambling sites he's visited and notifications from a body-building club he's part of. Tom has three-hundred-and-twenty-two *friends*. A few more *friends* than Zoe then.

Tom has several photos on his profile, but only one has Zoe in it. Tom has his arm around Zoe at some sort of a party. Zoe's wearing a silver, satin number and Tom's in a dinner jacket. Both are smiling at the camera but there's uneasiness in their pose. I can't quite place it, but they look awkward, as if it's an act they are putting on for the other partygoers.

The posts that are on Zoe's wall need to be deleted in case Tom sees them. I don't want him logging on and reading that she loves her life and her husband when it's simply not true in my case. The less I have to do with Tom the better and the less reason I give him to contact me the better. So, I return to her profile and delete the posts.

*

My head and eyes start to hurt. I've been looking at this computer screen for far too long now. It's now seven-thirty and I am starving.

Leaving the laptop on the bed I pop downstairs to ask Arthur for any takeaway menus he may have. I really fancy a pizza with all the extras. My body tells me I'm vegetarian, but my mind is firmly fixed in the world of meat.

I cough as I approach the last step so as not to startle Arthur again.

'Hello dear! How's the surfing going?' Arthur says.

'Hi Arthur,' I reply. 'It's going OK thank you. But I have to say I'm starving hungry now. I was wondering if you knew of any good takeaways that deliver here.'

'Aha, well what do you fancy? You can have Chinese, Indian, Italian, Thai, Fried Chick ...'

Bless him, he's so happy to help. I interrupt his list of menus. 'Thank you, Arthur, I was thinking of pizza actually.'

'Well, there's a lovely place, not far away that delivers, I'm sure I have a menu here somewhere. Give me two seconds and I'll pop out the back to have a look.'

There's a smell of food wafting from the back of the B&B. I can smell roast pork. It makes me feel sick I'm so hungry.

Arthur returns. 'Here you are dear, give them a ring, they're very tasty!'

'Thanks Arthur,' I say. I take the menu and return to my room.

The food arrives forty minutes later. The delivery man is accompanied by Arthur. I give the delivery man the cash left over from Tom's food shop.

Laying the food out on the bed, I realise I have ordered enough to feed a family of six. There's a fourteen-inch meaty pizza, garlic bread, wedges, coleslaw, barbecue sauce, four pieces of fried chicken and a bottle of coke. I feel like me again. I love my food, and can't wait to tuck in. I can feel my body fighting the urge to reject the meat but persevere. I will not let my new body come between me and the food I love and was born to eat.

Halfway through the food, my belly is close to bursting. One thing I can't change is the size of my new stomach. It's impossible to fit anything more into my skinny frame, so I collapse onto the bed with a groan.

*

After lying there for a good ten minutes, I feel able to move again. I tidy away the food, and re-open the laptop ready to log back into Facebook. This time I shall log in as me, Aisha Brown.

My profile is loaded with new notifications. It hasn't been touched for months, not since the accident. There are game requests, friends' updates, photos added by people and people's comments on other people's profiles.

There is a post on my wall from my mum saying:

Hello Aisha, how are you? I haven't spoken to you since you came home from hospital. I've tried calling but you won't answer. I'm worried. Please call me.

Gemma commented on my mum's post saying:

I know, it's like she's cut herself off, hasn't even been on here. I haven't heard from her either. Have tried speaking to Luke about it but he just says to give her time. What should we do?

Mum replies:

We're her family and she needs us. 'I'm going around there tonight, I'll let you know how I get on Gemma. Don't worry, she'll be OK.

My poor mum and Gemma, they must be going out of their minds with worry. I always spoke to mum once a week and wouldn't go without seeing Gemma for more than two days at a time. They must be wondering what's gotten into me. Zoe doesn't know what she's missing. My family are the best anyone could wish for. But at least she's not moving in on my family as well as my husband.

That was the last post from my mum and Gemma. A week has passed since mum said she was going to go around to mine and Luke's, and she hasn't said how it went. Perhaps she's spoken to Gemma on the phone since visiting.

It comes up on my profile that I'm married to Luke. So, like I did for Tom, I click on Luke Brown so that I can view his profile and recent activity.

There are a few posts from a few months ago saying his life was falling apart, he didn't know what to do, he was so worried. This must have been shortly after the accident.

The most recent posts say how everything is now wonderful, things couldn't be better, he's so happy. It feels as though someone has taken a knife, stabbed it in my chest and twisted round and round. Luke's happy. He's happy with *her*. She's happy with him. Where do I fit in? Nowhere, that's where. Well, that's going to change.

All of this afternoon's knowledge gives me more determination than ever to get some answers and find out a way of returning to my old life. There will be knock-backs I'm sure and upset along the way, but I will succeed and regain my identity. I am Aisha Brown, and I will get my life back.

I have always had in the back of my mind that if both I and Zoe really want our lives back; we will find a way. But now I know she doesn't want to reclaim her life back from me.

So, I must do this alone. I must fight for what is rightfully mine. First thing's first. Tomorrow I will speak to my husband.

12

It's ten-thirty on Saturday morning and I'm sat in the back seat of a taxi, outside my house. The rain is pelting down on the windscreen, and the wipers are working at brushing off the drops.

The meter reads five pounds forty. I ask the driver to keep the meter running and wait for me. I can't imagine I will be long. I step out of the car under my umbrella. My stomach still feels sore and tender after this morning.

My stomach acted as my alarm at five-thirty this morning. I had to rush out of bed to the bathroom to throw-up. Thirty minutes I was in there hugging the toilet bowl retching until there was nothing left to bring up. Perhaps eating so much, so late took its toll on my new slim line, vegetarian frame. My head didn't regret finishing off the food at eleven-thirty last night, I enjoyed every mouthful. But my body was screaming at me this morning, punishing me.

When I was there, crouched around the toilet bowl in the early hours of this morning, I longed for my mum or Luke to come in and hold my hair back for me whilst rubbing my back. They were both so good when I was poorly. They would always look after me and I would feel better in no time. But it was just me this morning. Not for long though I thought as I clambered up off the bathroom floor. Staring in the mirror, I told myself, this is it. Time to get your life back Aisha.

And here I am, outside my house, in the pouring rain doing just that. I have no idea what I'm going to say or do, especially if *she* answers the door. I hope and pray Luke is in and I can speak to him. I must make him believe me; I must prove to him what I say is the truth. But I know how it will make me sound. He will think I am a mad woman. But I must try.

Our house looks exactly the same from the outside. The garden gate joins to a path which leads all the way up to the front door. Either side of the path are flowers I planted myself. Of course, being September, they were starting to die off now, but they still looked pretty. I was never green-fingered, but since buying our first house, I tried some gardening and picked some beautiful bedding plants for the front garden. There were geraniums, hydrangeas and snapdragons and either side of the front door were two hanging baskets full of pretty bedding plants.

My mobile starts to vibrate in my bag. I rummage quickly for it before it starts ringing too loudly drawing attention to me. It's Tom again. He's already tried calling me twice this morning. I can't speak to him, especially not now, outside my house, just before I go and speak to my husband. I cut him off then turn the phone off.

The garden gate creaks as I open it. It's funny, I've never noticed that before, but when you're trying to be quiet, the slightest sound seems much louder. I walk up the path and approach the chestnut door. We always forgot to replace the doorbell battery, so it never worked so instead, I rattle the letterbox.

My pulse is quickening and even though it's cool outside in the rain, beads of sweat form on my brow and my hands start to get clammy. I close my eyes in anticipation.

The door opens and it's Gemma. 'May I help you?' She asks.

I would never have thought it would be Gemma standing in my front porch greeting me. I try to hide the surprise from my face, swallow and take a deep breath.

'Hello, I was looking for Luke Brown please,' I just about manage.

A look of suspicion crosses over Gemma's face. 'Can I ask who's asking please?' She says.

OK, what do I say? I wasn't planning on Gemma answering the door. Well, I wasn't planning anything really. Seeing her again makes me just want to hug her and squeeze her so tightly and tell her I've missed her. But I stop myself.

'I'm an old friend,' I say. It's the first thing that pops into my head. Probably not the best thing to say, but I go with it.

She looks at me quizzically and says, 'OK, I'll go and get him for you.'

She closes the door so that just a small gap remains open. I can hear her shout for Luke and tell him it's an old friend for him at the door.

An old friend, I'm more than an old friend, I'm his wife. But I couldn't really say that to Gemma, she'd sure as anything slam the door in my face and call me crazy.

My head turns up to above the front door. This house was mine and Luke's dream house. We saved for years whilst renting a grotty, damp-filled cottage. Then finally with some help from our parents we managed to scrape together a deposit to put down on this house.

On our first night in our new house, with boxes lying all around us, we ordered a Chinese takeaway and munched our way through it, sat on the floor of our lounge with TV plugged in and a sole lamp switched on. We felt so content. We had done it. We'd managed to buy our very own house; one we could call our own and do what we liked to. We could now plan things like dinner parties and barbeques.

That first night, we talked about starting a family now that we had the room. There were two bedrooms in our new house, one of which would be wonderful as a nursery to start and then a little child's bedroom in the future. We'd wanted to do things traditionally, get married, buy a house and then try for a family. We just knew there were good times ahead, now it was a case of making it happen.

I hear footsteps approaching the front door and my pulse quickens again. I take a deep breath, what am I going to say? I decide the only thing I can do is be honest and if that means he slams the door in my face, so be it, at least, I hope, I would give him something to think about.

The door pulls open. 'May I help you?' Luke asks.

There he is my husband, as beautiful as ever. He's wearing jeans and the t-shirt I bought for him last Christmas. His dark hair is stylishly messy, and he is waiting for my response, blue eyes expectant.

'Hello,' I start. 'Do you recognise me?'

Luke pauses and says, 'Yes, yes I do, I bumped into you whilst shopping and you fainted. Um… how are you?'

Of course, I forgot he would recognise me from the supermarket. 'Yes, I'm OK thank you, thanks for helping me that day I was very confused, and a bit startled.'

'OK, well, I must ask what brings you here. And how did you know where I live?' He says.

I take a deep breath and blurt it out. 'Right, well you're not going to believe me, but I have to speak to you. I know you Luke, I know you very well. I know you probably better than anyone else in the world. I don't know what happened to me, how I got into this mess, but I need your help.'

Luke frowns and scratches his head ruffling his brown locks. 'I'm sorry miss, but I don't know who you are. I can't help you, I'm sorry.' He goes to shut the door, but I wedge my foot in-between it and the door frame. The door crushes my foot, but I don't feel any pain.

'Please,' I say. 'You need to understand. Luke, I was in a terrible accident in July this year and I ended up in a coma. I woke up to find that my life had been taken from me. The husband I married wasn't by my bedside, but a total stranger was, claiming to be my husband.'

Luke begins to open the door again slowly. I continue, 'I was told by the doctors that it was all in my head, my dreams during the coma had gotten mixed up with my memories. But then I saw you Luke, at the supermarket. And I knew then that it really did happen. Somehow I switched bodies and lives with a girl called Zoe.'

Luke stops me. 'Um… I don't quite understand what you're saying miss. Do you need me to call someone? A doctor maybe?'

'No, no don't you see. Luke, it's me, Aisha.'

The colour drains from Luke's face. I can see the colour fade from pink to grey. His eyes narrow and across his beautiful face a darker, angrier expression forms.

'I would like you to leave now please.' He is calm in how he says it, but I can tell inside he is seething. I know that tone of voice so well, but he has never used it on me before. 'I don't want to have to ask you again.'

I start to panic. This isn't going the way I'd hoped. I have to make him believe me; I need him. Zoe is living my life but not for much longer if I can help it.

'Is she here? Zoe or Aisha or whatever she's calling herself. Where is she? She knows what's happening because she's going through it too. I know she is.' I try to peer around the door, desperately trying to see if she's there somewhere, listening. But I can't see past Luke.

'She's not here, and even if she was, do you really think I'd let her see you? She's going through a lot at the moment and she doesn't need a crazy woman turning up at her door saying all these ludicrous things.' Luke says.

Gemma reappears at the door. She's obviously been listening in. 'I really think you should go now. You've obviously got some issues and need help. But, quite frankly, I don't care. All I care about is the man stood next to me. This man also doesn't need you turning up here, saying all this stuff!'

The two people I care most about in the world are stood here in front of me, not knowing who I am. It's infuriating! Why can't they see it's possible?

'Gemma, please it's me, Aish! Can't you see? I know I look different, but it *is* me.'

I can see Gemma's right hand now and in it is a phone. 'I'm going to call the police if you don't leave right now,' she says.

What can I do? I must prove to them it's me, somehow.

'OK, OK,' I say. 'But please, just think about what I've said. It's not impossible, I can vouch for that. I can prove it, Luke, I bought you those clothes for Chri ...'

To avoid injury to my foot, I remove it sharply as the door is slammed in my face.

Back in the taxi, I stare out of the window at the house of our dreams and can see those dreams melting away. The driver starts to pull away, but I stop him.

'Stop a second please, Drive,' I say. 'Do you have a pen and something to write on?'

The driver huffs and digs around in his glove box. He pulls out a pen and a napkin, probably from his drive-through earlier today.

I thank him and scrawl down my number and a note on the napkin:

If you want to hear more, please contact me. I'll be waiting for you.

Aisha x

Leaving the taxi once more, I dart through the rain back to the front door and drop the note through the letterbox. This is just the first hurdle. There will be more I know, but at some point, there will be a finish line, and I will make them see it's me. That is all I can do today. Now I must wait.

13

Back in my B&B room, I feel so small in the big world. I sit on the bed and think of the look on Luke's face as I told him who I was. The anger and confusion he showed hurt me. I never thought he would look at me the way he did today. But then he doesn't realise what's happened, he doesn't believe what I told him. I hope that I haven't upset him or caused him pain or misery. I had to speak to him. I had to tell him. Even if nothing comes of it, I have tried. But I will not give up now.

It really took me by surprise that Gemma was there. That, I was not expecting. I'm pleased that Luke has Gemma though. Perhaps Zoe was injured as badly as me and has been leaning on Gemma for a bit more support.

I still have the laptop Arthur kindly lent to me. I never did manage to read the rest of that news article about my car crash, due to Tom ripping it up in front of me. Perhaps there are some reports online?

In Google, I type *Zoe Young car accident July 2012* and it brings up the news article I had started reading, along with a number of other reports from different newspapers. I read the article.

COMA GIRL'S 'SECRET' LIFE

Zoe Young, 30, of Taunton, was discharged from hospital today after a three-week stay. Insiders tell us that Mrs Young has been undergoing psychiatric help after emerging from a coma with amnesia. She remembers nothing of her life with her husband, Tom, but believes she has led a completely different life from the one she has woken up to.

A head-on collision, which occurred at 14.30 on July 22, resulted in Mrs Young's two-day coma. It is reported the driver of the other car, Mrs Aisha Brown, 30, also awoke from a two-day coma and was seriously injured. However, she has not needed any psychiatric help.

The car crash has been called a tragic accident with no suspicions pinned on either driver. Both women are recovering well although both have been suffering with confusion and memory loss.

One source explains that Mrs Young was so confused that she did not recognise her husband and was claiming she was Aisha Brown. The source continues to say that it was so distressing to watch her push away her husband who clearly adored her and had been so worried about her.

Mrs Young has since realised during her stay at a rehabilitation unit, that her memories have become confused with the dreams she had during her coma. She is now on her way to a full recovery and has returned to her home in Taunton with husband Tom Young.

So, Zoe was also in a coma, just like me. But she didn't need any psychiatric help. So, did she just wake up and think it was great to have a new husband and new life? I don't understand how someone could wake up like I did and not feel the same way. Unless she couldn't remember anything, which is possible, as the article states she also suffered from memory loss. However, surely if she had no memory, she would receive some support of some kind to help her rebuild it.

My mind starts working overtime. Perhaps she woke up with no memory, then shortly regained it but preferred the new life she had woken up in to her one with Tom. Maybe she then agreed with everything she was being told, needed no extra help from the doctors and if she slipped up at all, she would blame it on her memory.

Who knows, this is just speculation. I won't get any answers unless I speak to her myself, which is not something I'm keen to do, at least not right now.

There are other news articles, most of which say the same kind of thing. They talk about me losing my memory, being confused, thinking I'd switched lives, then getting better and living happily ever after with Tom.

I type in *Aisha Brown car accident* into Google to see if this brings up anything different. I can't believe what I find. She has written a blog. It's a first-person account of the car accident, from *her* point of view. I compose myself before reading.

RE-BORN

I am writing this to try and help me regain all of my memories from before the car accident. I hope that those who know me, who read this, will understand why I need to write it down.

On July 22nd my car hit another, and my world changed, for the better. You see, I was happy enough living my life and doing all of the day-to-day meaningless things. But I never knew what could be and how things could be even better.

There are still many gaps in my memory which day by day I am filling. My husband Luke and my best friend Gemma have been a fantastic support to me. I never appreciated a loving husband or a close friend before, but now, now that they are here, I will never lose them.

I remember being married before the accident, but I don't remember the wedding day. It's sad that I can't remember marrying such a wonderful man, but I have seen the pictures and will treasure them forever. In the pictures we both look so happy and in love. I need that love and am grateful to have found it.

When my car hit another in July, I fell into a two-day coma. When I finally woke, Luke was there by my side, holding my hand. I'll be honest; I didn't recognise him at first. I didn't know who he was, and I had no idea what had happened to me. The doctors told me I had been in a serious accident and had suffered a blow to the head and broken at least three ribs. I'd obviously lost my memory. I panicked and lashed out, for which I am terribly sorry. But Luke forgave me.

The doctors told me I was lucky. I was resuscitated after my heart stopped on the operating table. I will forever be in debt to the doctors who saved me.

My family welcomed me into their arms. I felt so lucky to have such loving parents. They now mean the world to me. I'm sure they always did, but after all their support and what I've put them through, I value them more now than I could possibly have done before. You take your life and your family for granted. You don't know what you have until you almost lose it.

I've turned vegetarian after the accident. I don't know why, but my tastes have changed and eating meat makes me vomit. Perhaps being meat-free will help lose some of the inches around my midriff I've gained over the years.

A frightening thing happened the other night, I felt like I was choking and unable to breathe. I'd forgotten I was asthmatic. It was thanks to Luke that I didn't suffer a major attack as he came running to me with my inhaler.

I'm gradually adjusting to my new life, the life after the accident. I call it my new life as everything has changed. I'm learning new things about myself every day and the more I learn, the happier I become.

For those of you who know me, but I have yet to see since the accident, please get in contact with me. There are so many people I have forgotten, but it seems that when I see them again, some memories do come back.

My final words today go to the lady who crashed into my car. I thank you for giving me a new perspective on things, for making me realise how lucky I am and for giving me a new lease of life. I died at that hospital and was re-born. I hope that you have also made a full recovery and are as happy with your life as I am with mine.

Here it is in black and white. Zoe Young is living and loving my life. My theory was correct. She is pretending to be suffering from amnesia, but I know the truth. She didn't like her own life, so when she was given a chance at a new life, my life, she took it. Well, I'm going to take it back.

How dare she thank me for crashing into her car? She must have known I would research the car accident and find her blog. I feel like adding a comment to the bottom of it, but I stop myself. I don't want to draw any more attention to myself, especially after meeting Luke this morning.

No wonder she can't remember the wedding day, she wasn't there, I was. It was me who made those vows to stand by Luke for richer, for poorer, in sickness and in health, until death do us part. And he made them to me, not her.

I suddenly feel worried and concerned for all those I love. I haven't thought about it this way before. They have a complete stranger living with them. Who knows what she could do? She may be a psychopath, a compulsive thief, a murderer! That may be a little extreme, I don't think Zoe is any of those things from what I know of her, but I do know she's a liar. And that in itself is a dangerous thing.

She makes a remark about my weight. So, she's skinny and a fitness freak. Well, I'm not. I like the comfortable things in life. I always wanted to lose weight, tried every diet under the sun, but the thing is I love my food. Now I'm stuck with her wafer-thin body, which I hate, and she's got my blubber which she wants to lose. I can't help but feel she's making a dig at me. Reading between the lines, she's saying I'm fat and she's going to lose the weight for me, which will be so easy for her and I should have lost the weight ages ago. Well, I'll let her carry on, at least when I get my body and life back, she'll have done the dieting for me. I suppose there are some positives to the situation.

Reading her story makes me feel terribly home sick. Not just for Luke and Gemma, but for my parents. I miss them so much. No wonder she is happy, my parents are great. Anyone would be lucky growing up with parents like mine. It's sad that she lost both of her parents, but now she's taken mine and she's not ashamed of it either.

Visiting Luke didn't work. Convincing him that I have changed bodies with Zoe Young will be difficult. Perhaps my parents will see through it. I shall rest for the remainder of the day and then tomorrow I will go and visit them. Surely, they will know their daughter when I turn up at their door. Families have their own in-jokes, silly little memories and sayings that no-one else understands. If they give me enough time to talk, they will see it's me. Even through this alien exterior, they have to know it's me.

14

For the first time since staying at the B&B I wake in a cold sweat. My nightmares have returned.

It's three o'clock on Sunday morning and I wake myself up yelling, but Tom isn't here to comfort me. The dream is similar to the ones I've had before. I have the stereo playing full blast and pull up to the junction. I'm crying hysterically.

In my past dreams, I've had people in the car with me, mum, dad, Luke, Gemma and Tom have all featured in my nightmares. This time I am on my own in the car. As I pull out of the junction, I see another car hurtling towards me. I try to put my foot on the brake quickly, but there isn't enough time. The car hits me. My car is spinning with me in it.

The car comes to a stop and my eyes begin to focus. Unlike my previous dreams, I'm not torn in half. I am whole and, in my arms, I am holding a baby.

There is some sudden clarity. All my nightmares have featured something to do with a baby. Something I haven't got. I suddenly have an overwhelming feeling of sadness. I won't ever have a baby. I don't know how I know this. I can only imagine it has something to do with what happened before the accident.

I close my eyes forcing myself to forget the dream and brush away the thought of being infertile. It can't be true. I won't let it. I force myself to sleep again but pray its dream-free.

*

My dad was a character. Anyone who ever met him fell in love with his humour and love of life. He was a wonderful father growing up, sitting me on his knee, bouncing me up and down, singing nursery rhymes. My mother was loving and kind, always being the one to cuddle me and offer me her love.

All my childhood, through to my teens I couldn't have wished for better parents. They always knew what to do and when. If I was upset, they would comfort me, if I was naughty, I knew it, and if I was happy, they'd share in my joy.

Seeing my house yesterday re-affirms my gratitude to my parents. Without them, we would never have been able to afford to move into our own home. There have been so many things they have helped me with financially over the years. They paid for me to study at private school, funded my university fees by themselves and even paid our first few months' rent at our old cottage.

It wasn't just big things they paid for. It was the little things that always meant so much. They would make sure Santa came every year and delivered some, if not most, of the presents on my list. If I had friends over for tea, they would go out of their way with the dinner, there'd always be plenty to eat and my friends never wanted to go home. Every summer, my parents would always make sure we went away on holiday somewhere, whether it be abroad or down to Cornwall.

I wasn't spoilt as a child though. I was fully aware of how hard my parents worked to be able to give me these things.

They taught me the phrase *I want won't get* and if I wanted something, I was often told no. But that was how it worked. I knew when I was pushing it, and they knew when I deserved something extra special.

Both of my parents were Christian. I was brought up in the Church and my faith grew over the years. I knew there was more to life and that every moment in life was a steppingstone towards the new one. Some people didn't understand my faith along the way or my parents', but I became stronger just as my faith did. I learnt that everyone has a right to believe what they want, no matter what religion and should they choose not to believe anything, then that's their choice.

It's nearing the afternoon and the dream I had last night resurfaces. I always told myself that when I have a child of my own, I want to bring them up as well as my parents raised me. I would love them dearly but not give in to their demands easily. I would want to raise them up in the Christian faith and I would want them to have morals and values the same as I did.

I want to have the chance of being as good a parent as mum and dad. I can't believe that this isn't the case, that I'm infertile. It was a dream, nothing else. It wasn't a memory; it can't have been. But it seemed so clear to me. I was awake when I felt that sadness; I did remember something.

My hopes of having a child of my own one day can't be taken from me. I have to believe that I will become a mother. I try to forget last night and think about today.

My mobile rings. Then, I realise that it can only be one person. There's only one person who knows me well enough as Zoe to call me.

I answer it hesitantly, 'Hello Tom.'

'Zoe, I'm going out of my mind! I tried calling you yesterday, but you didn't answer, thank God you've answered now. Are you OK?'

Tom genuinely sounds worried and concerned. I soften and feel a bit bad for what I've put him through. 'I'm alright Tom, sorry to make you worry, I'm getting there.'

'Well of course I'm going to worry Zoe. You're my wife! When are you coming home?' Tom says.

I try to explain as best I can without telling Tom too much. 'I'm not ready yet Tom. I'm sorry. My head's still all over the place, and I need answers. When I get those answers then maybe… maybe I will be ready.'

'Oh Zoe. You do make me worry. I love you. I just want you to know that.'

Deep down, I know that he does. That's what makes me feel so bad, as how can I say that back to him? I can't. As far as I'm concerned, I've only just met him and am in love with someone else.

'I know you do Tom,' I say. 'That's why you need to let me do this. The more you hassle me, the further you'll push me. If you love me as you say you do, you'll be patient with me.'

Tom sighs down the phone. 'I am being patient Zoe. I am. At least I'm trying to be. But we really do need to talk soon. It's important.'

'Well, if it's important, can't you tell me now whilst we're on the phone?' I suddenly feel the need to wrap this up, I've got things to do and parents to see. 'Actually Tom, I'm really quite busy, can we do this another time please?'

'It's not something I want to talk to you about on the phone. I need to see you. Please think about a time we can meet.' He says.

'Look Tom, I'll call you tonight.' I know if I don't call him, he'll only keep ringing me.

'Do you promise? Please? I'll be waiting.' Tom replies.

'I promise Tom, I'll call you at seven.' With that I hang up.

*

My parents live five miles away from the B&B. I'm sure I will become a regular taxi customer. Seeing as Zoe has money to spare, it saves me from getting the bus. After my last experience travelling on public transport, I feel more comfortable sat in the back of a taxi. No strange women sitting next to me whilst I'm trying to conceal the tears flowing down my face. That lady has stayed with me though. Even though she was incredibly annoying, what she said keeps running through my mind.

Keep following your path but look out for side roads. Don't let them pass you by.

Everyone has a path through life. I am a great believer in this. There is one main road, but you can choose to branch off, down other avenues. Which ones you choose can play an important part in your journey through life. But at some point, no matter what side roads you take, the satnav of life will always re-calculate and take you back onto that main road.

This is another side road I will not let pass me by. Who knows where it will take me? But I know whatever happens, I will return to my destined path.

It's the same taxi driver as yesterday. He doesn't particularly look pleased to see me. I did keep him waiting for a while yesterday and I will today as well I expect. However, at least he gets a good fare out of me each time.

Thankfully there is no rain today. The sun is shining and rather hot for this time in September. My jumper has to come off, my temperature is rising. It's warm in the back of the taxi but mix this with the nervousness of being turned away by my parents and it's enough to send anyone over boiling point.

Ten minutes later the taxi parks up outside my childhood home. My parents never moved. I was born in this house and lived there until I was eighteen. I don't think they will ever move now. Not unless they're forced to when they're older due to too much maintenance.

The house is situated on an acre of land, the size of half a football pitch. The gardens are immaculately kept with an array of different fruit trees I used to pick from as a child. My tree house is no longer there. It rotted a number of years ago, so my dad had to take it down.

Their car is parked outside which means they are in. I made sure I waited until I knew they would be back from church and already eaten their Sunday roast. I wonder to myself what they had today. I used to love their roast lamb on a Sunday. They would put rosemary on it which tasted divine.

I walk up the gravel path to the front door, hands shaking as I approach the doorbell. I ring once.

My dad's voice is heard getting closer to the door and I can hear him asking my mum who it could be. The latch is drawn back, and the door opened.

There he is, my father, as broad and lovely as ever. He's greying slightly but still has his mop of light brown hair. His beard needs a trim again though. It's at the point where it's starting to look messy, as if food is being collected in amongst the hairs. I used to take the mick out of dad when his beard got to that state, saying he looked like a farmer.

Dad looks quizzically towards me. But then, I am stood there gawping at him and smiling slightly ludicrously at his chin.

'Hello?' Dad snaps me out of my lingering stare.

'Oh hello, my name's Zoe Young, I was hoping to speak to your daughter Aisha Brown.' I've decided to try a different tactic from how I dealt with Luke and Gemma.

My dad gets a bit defensive, which I'm pleased about as it shows he's still protecting his daughter. 'She doesn't live here anymore. What business is she of yours?'

'I was the lady involved in the car crash. I was hoping she was OK and thought I'd see how she was. I also wanted to apologise for crashing into her. Believe me when I tell you I didn't come out of it unscathed.'

My dad pauses, then says, 'I see. Well, as I said, she's not here I'm afraid.'

'I understand, but I must be honest, I've travelled quite a long way to come here,' I lie. 'I'm just trying to piece together what happened. It's a lot to deal with and I'm sure she's going through a lot right now too.'

My dad softens a little. 'Well, I've read some stories about the accident, and saw that you were in hospital too. Had a few injuries too didn't you? It was a terrible thing to have happened. But, like I said, she's not here.'

I think about how to get around this. 'I know I'm disturbing you and don't want to impose, but would you mind if I spoke to you about the accident? I'm just looking for some answers to all this confusion.'

'Don't you have any friends or family?' Dad asks.

I shake my head. 'No. I have a husband, but since the accident, we've been having a few issues, so we're currently separated.'

He replies, 'Well I'm really not sure how much help I'll be ...'

'Anything … anything at all you can help me with. I've not been the same since the accident and I don't have anyone else to talk to about it.'

I can see my dad start to soften. I know both of my parents so well and know that with a bit of persistence on my part they wouldn't want to turn away someone in need, not even a stranger.

'OK … well … Would you like a cup of tea?' He says.

That would be utterly amazing I think to myself. How wonderful, a cuppa in my parents' house, in my parent's kitchen and with *my* parents. 'Yes please,' I say. 'That would be lovely.'

We sit at the wooden kitchen table. Mum has joined us and pours the tea from the teapot. She offers me sugar, so take three teaspoonfuls. I only have sweet tea when I'm feeling particularly anxious, and today I feel as though I deserve extra sweetening-up. I catch my mum giving me a glance as I scoop the sugar into my cup.

'Sorry,' I say. 'I always have extra 'taste' in my tea when I'm feeling a bit … overwhelmed. Thank you.'

Mum casts dad a confused look. She looks exactly the same. Glasses perched on the end of her nose and jet-black hair waving down around her face. She could give the best cuddles and right now that's all I wanted her to do.

'Right then, what is it you want to know?' Dad starts by saying.

OK, I hadn't thought about what to say once I was inside.

'Well, mainly just how she is after the accident. Has anything changed?' I ask.

My mum shifts in her seat and rubs her nose. 'She's not been herself since the accident,' mum says. 'She's cut herself off from us sadly. We used to talk all the time but now...'

Mum starts to blub. She pulls a handkerchief from her pocket and blows her nose.

'Sorry,' she says. 'It's been an exceedingly difficult time for us all. Dave and I were only saying the other day that she's changed. I can't tell how exactly. It's like she left something behind in that car, woke up a completely different woman. She doesn't call us; she doesn't see us and it's as if we don't exist to her anymore.'

Dad rescues mum by saying, 'What Carol is trying to say is Aisha used to be so close to us. We would speak to her at least once a week. Since the accident, we've only spoken to her once. That's once in two months. And that was the day she came out of hospital.'

'Can I be honest with you both,' I ask. 'I've felt the same way as Aisha. I don't feel like the same person, in fact I'm not the same person as I was before the car accident. I think more than the cars collided that day. I believe we collided, me and Aisha.'

They both stare at me and then they stare at each other.

My dad turns back to me and says, 'What is it you're trying to say exactly?'

Here goes. 'I believe that when our cars crashed, we were both plunged into darkness at the same time, and our bodies switched or our souls switched, whichever way you want to look at it. I believe I'm your daughter. I believe I'm Aisha.'

15

The response was not exactly what I'd wanted. My parents thought I was completely insane. I won't be invited back there again. I still had half a cup of tea left when my dad ushered me out of the house. They were very polite about how they kicked me out. They could never be rude or cruel, but they wanted me out. I could tell. So, I let my dad show me the door.

Part of me now knows that they don't see me in Aisha anymore. They know that she's changed, and perhaps once they've thought about what I've said it will start to make more sense to them. Maybe that's just me hoping, but there's a chance.

I treasure the fact that they took the time to speak to me. Just that brief encounter with my parents makes me feel better.

I don't feel as sad as I thought I would when they turned me away. I've had enough knock backs now to cope with this one. I am just pleased to have seen them. I'm pleased to know they are well, but I feel sorry for them. Zoc hasn't treated them well and there's nothing I can do about it. Not at the moment anyway.

It's almost seven o'clock. I have to ring Tom. But first, I need to return the laptop to Arthur, I've had it for over two days now, other guests may need to borrow it. I take it down to him at reception, but he tells me not to worry about it. No-one else needs it at the moment, so I can keep it. He will let me know when he needs it again.

Back in my room, I pull out my mobile from my pocket. There are no missed calls, so Tom kept his word and has patiently waited for my call. I'd better keep my promise to him and give him a ring.

There are two rings and Tom picks up. 'Thanks for calling me love.'

'That's OK, I did promise,' I say.

'How has your day been?' Tom's trying to start a normal conversation with me. What do I say? I woke up this morning after being rejected by both my husband and best friend, and now I have been turned away by both of my parents. It's been just another day in my mixed-up life.

'It's been OK thanks Tom. I've been keeping myself busy with this and that.'

He pauses, 'I miss you Zoe.'

I can't keep going over the same thing with him each time we talk. 'I know you do. We can't keep going around in circles though Tom, I need time. But I'm happy to meet up with you now, I feel ready.'

'Oh, that's great! Thank you so much love, can we meet tomorrow? I can take you for lunch or dinner?' He says.

It's far too soon to be sitting down for a meal again with Tom. I'm happy to meet up with him, but I'm not ready for the awkward meal silences.

The last meal I ate with Tom was the night before we were planning on going to Cheddar Gorge. He'd gone all out and made Zoe's favourite dish of vegetarian lasagna and salad.

He'd even bought us a bottle of non-alcoholic wine to share. I think back to that meal. I could have done with some alcohol to get me through the awkwardness. When you've been with someone a while, you learn to enjoy the silences you have between you. It doesn't matter if neither of you talks, you're just happy in each other's company.

This was not the case with Tom. Every mouthful was chewed down in tense silence. But due to now supposedly being a health freak, I wasn't allowed to touch alcohol. Tom had told me it wasn't good for my health. He said it made you gain weight and that was something I did not want to start doing. Apparently, it was important for me to stay in shape and if that meant not touching alcohol then I didn't.

There is no way I'm eating with him tomorrow. 'Can we meet for a coffee? I've not been particularly hungry lately, I've been very fussy about what I eat, so wouldn't want to waste money there. There's a coffee place called Bumbles shall we meet there at eleven tomorrow?'

'I know it,' He says. 'I'll be there waiting for you.'

We say our goodbyes. I'm not so hasty to hang up this time. He's not a bad man, I can see that. Zoe picked a good one when she went husband fishing.

*

Two minutes after I ended the conversation with Tom my phone rings again. What now? I've agreed to meet up with him, tomorrow, what more does he want?

I pick the phone up, but it's not Tom. It's a number I don't recognise. No-one else has ever called me on this phone before. Perhaps it's a market research company or my phone provider. I used to get pestered by both on my old phone.

An old client once told me a story about her winning a battle with conservatory salesmen. She received a sales call one day and showed incredible enthusiasm in response to all their sales pitches. They asked her if she'd ever considered having a conservatory. To which she replied that she'd always wanted one. They told her all the different options of make, colour and size. She ended up keeping them on the phone for over half-an-hour, until finally they thought they had the sale in the bag. They asked her if she would like to go ahead with the deal. She replied that she would love to. Knowing that she had sufficiently wasted their time she explained that there was one slight technicality. She lived in a second floor flat.

Holding the phone in my hand, I hesitantly answer it.

'Hello?' I say.

'Can I speak to Zoe please?' It's a female voice which is very familiar.

My heart starts to pound. 'Gemma, is that you?'

There is a short silence. 'Yes, yes, it is. I thought I'd give you a quick call as I couldn't stop thinking about what you said yesterday.'

She got my note and number. And she wants to speak to me. This could be a breakthrough. The one I've been waiting and longing for. My best friend knows who I am. I knew I could rely on Gemma to see through the exterior.

'Gemma!' I cry. 'You got my note! Thank you so much for calling me.'

'Well, I'm not going to keep you long,' she says. 'Luke doesn't know I'm ringing you. He'd kill me if he did. You know, he's very upset about you turning up like that.'

'I can imagine. I dealt with it all wrong. I shouldn't have just blurted it out like that. But you have to believe me Gemma. You and me, we're soul mates, always have been, always will be,' I say.

'Look, I'm really not sure what to believe,' she says. 'I mean, what you're saying, it's impossible. You can't just switch bodies. I don't know who you are, you're a stranger, yet somehow you do seem familiar. What I do know is that, Aish, she hasn't been the same since the crash. She's … well, different.'

That's because she's not Aisha, I am. 'Does this mean you think it's possible?'

This could be too good to be true. My pulse is beating ten-to-the-dozen. Please say it's possible. Please believe it could be true.

'I don't know,' she says. 'Look, I think we should meet. Talk things through, see in person if I think you could be telling the truth.'

That's great! She'll know it's me in no time if we sit down together, like old times. 'When?' I manage to say through my excitement.

Gemma says, 'No time like the present. We can meet in the bar near my work. You'll know where that is if you are Aisha, or if you've done your homework well. See you in half an hour?'

'I'll be there,' I say. 'Thanks for giving me the chance.'

*

The emotions I feel are strange. I have never felt nervous to see my best friend before. I would normally get excited about seeing her, every time. It didn't matter what we were doing. Whether we were going Christmas shopping or just hanging around at either of our places, we would always have something to say and have something to giggle about.

Gemma was present at every major event of my life. She was there on my eighteenth birthday when I was crying over Ben Matthews dumping me. When I graduated from university, she came to watch the ceremony. It was at her birthday party that I met my future husband, and it was her who woke up next to me on the day of my wedding.

She must know who I am. All she has to do is look into my eyes and she'll know it's me. I almost made a breakthrough with my parents, if I can convince Gemma that what happened is true, then others may start to believe me too.

One time in school, we fell out. It was a pretty bad falling-out as it lasted four days. Neither of us spoke to each other, but to this day we can't remember what it was that caused us to fall out. The way we finally made up was by me making her a mixtape of all our favourite songs. The songs we used to play and dance to at sleepovers, the ones that always caused us to laugh and have fun together.

We knew each other so well. If we fell out, it never lasted long, as one of us would always find a way of making the other person smile. Once one of us smiled, there was no going back, we were mates again.

I enter The Pitcher and Piano. I knew instantly which bar she meant. The one near the school she and Luke work at. We'd go there quite a lot as they had deals on double vodkas and double martinis. I hope Luke doesn't know. From what

Gemma said earlier, Luke wouldn't be impressed if he knew she was meeting me, and I wouldn't want him to be angry with her.

My watch says seven-forty. We said on the phone we'd meet in half an hour, which means seven-forty-five. There's no sign of her yet so I order us both a drink, double martini and lemonade for Gemma and a double vodka and coke for me. I carry them over to a table by the window and wait.

It's tempting to down my vodka in one as I'm so nervous. But I resist the urge as I want her to see the drinks I've ordered as her first sign that I'm telling her the truth. Time is ticking by, so I pick the cocktail menu up to read. It gives me something to do with my itching fingers.

'Aisha?' I hear in my left ear. I drop the menu on the table and look up with a beaming grin on my face. But it's not her.

She's been out in the sun too much; I can tell as her freckles cover her whole face.

16

'What are you doing here? I … I was expecting Gemma,' I say.

I can't believe Zoe is here. Can I please have a break from all these unpleasant surprises?   At first, I feel disappointment like I've never felt before and then it turns to anger. 'How dare you turn up like this? If I'd wanted to see you, I'd have asked to see you. Gemma will be here in a bit, we're going to try and sort things out, and so I suggest you leave now.'

'Gemma's not coming,' she says. 'She told me she was coming to meet you. Let's just say, I reassured her that you were fresh out of the loony bin and couldn't be trusted.'

How dare she do this? She's taken so much already. She just keeps twisting the knife.

This is the first time I've properly seen Zoe up close. I saw her that day in the supermarket, but I didn't want to look too closely. Looking at her now, it's like looking in the mirror. She's kept my hair long and has it scraped back in a ponytail today. She's obviously gotten used to wearing my contacts as she's not wearing glasses. The only notable difference is that I can see she's lost weight. She's losing *my* weight. She's taking my body to the gym and toning it up.

I actually feel quite abused. It's my body, and someone else shouldn't be taking this much notice of how it looks. It's like sharing me with a stranger. She's seen me naked! The thought only just dawns on me. The only person who has seen me naked for the last five years is Luke. I feel violated. She obviously didn't like what she saw so she's changing it.

She's standing there as bold as brass. I need to use this situation to my advantage. I need to see if she remembers anything about the accident, if she knows where I was heading before we crashed and ask her outright why she wants my life so much over her own.

'Do you know why we crashed?' I ask her. 'I need to know. You have to tell me if you know anything.'

'I don't have to tell you anything,' she smirks. 'But I do know you were on your way back from the doctors. I received a letter once I got out of hospital which had a leaflet in it about premature ovarian failure. It looks like you were distracted. So, if there's anyone to blame for the accident, it's you.'

Premature ovarian failure? I was right. The nightmares I'd been having were really memories trying to resurface. I can't have children. She has no right opening my letters. Does Luke know? He obviously wasn't with me as he wasn't in the accident. What if she has told Luke because I never got the chance? I won't let her see how upset I am by the news.

'Why, Zoe?' I ask. 'Why are you doing this? You have your own life, with Tom. I can see you're so happy living mine, but why? I don't know how this happened, but surely you can't feel that happy about it all. Don't you want things to go back to how they were?'

She snorts. 'You have no idea about me. Have you taken the time to get to know my life and how bleak and miserable it was? All I had was Tom, my work and my bank balance. I had no friends, no family.'

'You have …' She laughs. 'Sorry *had* it all Aisha, but you lost it. I have no desire to go back to that life. If there is a way to get it back, I want no part in it.'

'Well then I'll have to find a way on my own Zoe,' I say. 'And believe me when I say, I will. They'll realise who you are, and then where will that leave you?'

'They won't Aisha. How could someone believe it's you when you look like me,' she says.

'I don't want *your* life. I want mine back!' She is really starting to wind me up.

'What? Even though you can't have kids. You should be *happy* with my life,' she says.

She continues. 'Tom's a good catch, he'll treat you right, he used to bore me to death, but I think you'll like that. Luke on the other hand … you did well for yourself there didn't you? I'm not sure what he saw in you, mind. But it's OK; I'll get your body in order very soon. I've started a strict exercise regime.'

How dare she! What a bitch. I hate myself even more now knowing what used to be inside this body before me. 'If you don't like my body, then give it back to me!'

She laughs hysterically. 'Do you think, even if I could give it back to you, I would? If I gave up on this body, I'd have to lose everything else I've gained. No chance! I can lose weight in your body, but as Zoe, I can't gain friends or family.'

'What about the money?' I say. 'Luke and I don't have half the money you have in savings. You'll get bored and ...'

'Oh, don't you worry, I have a few plans underway. I'm paying for you to live the high life. Well don't get used to it. I'll get my money back. But I need to sort this out first,' she looks down at her body. 'How could Luke really love me looking like this?'

Her gaze falls to the alcohol in my glass, raises her eyebrows and says, 'Talking of bodies, should you really be drinking that?'

With that, I don't hold back. The martini I bought for Gemma gets thrown all over Zoe's face. 'I will find a way Zoe, with or without my body. I will get my life back.'

I walk towards the exit, head held high and hear her voice shouting after me, 'Best get a move on then Aisha, time's ticking!'

I turn around to see her raise her right index finger to her forehead and give me the same, threatening point she did in the supermarket that day. As I march out of the exit, I beat away the shivers running down my spine.

*

There was a time during my teens that I was bullied. I would come home from school and cry non-stop for hours, every night. My parents became very concerned and finally asked me why I didn't want to go in in the mornings. I told them that some of the girls were picking on me because of my weight. They called me things like *Pig Face* and *Fatty*. It was making my teenage years a misery.

That's when I started my first diet. I was fourteen years old and I needed to lose weight. I necded to feel better about myself and stop the bullies from targeting me. If I was slim then I thought they would stop.

Over two years I lost three stone and felt like a normal teenager. The bullying stopped for a while until they found something else to pick on. They chose my glasses. That's when I got contact lenses.

Image shouldn't be a big thing for children growing up. They should be happy in their own skin, but I never was. I would put on weight, lose it and then put it back on again. The first time I truly accepted myself was when I met Luke. He fell in love with me when I was at my biggest so I knew he would love me no matter what. Over the five years with Luke, I yo-yo dieted until I was at the weight I and my body felt comfortable with and this is where I stayed.

When I first looked in that full-length mirror in Tom's house, it was clear to me how much work Zoe did to keep her body in its perfect hour-glass shape. I'd never had a body like that before. Being Zoe, I feel tiny. When I was Aisha, I felt like a hulk next to everyone. Even at my slimmest, I still felt like the fat girl inside.

Seeing Zoe last night really opened my eyes. I could tell she'd lost weight, but I didn't feel tiny in comparison with her. I don't know if this is because I still feel like the fat girl inside, or if I wasn't as big as I thought before the accident. But her comments still hurt.

I think I've put on some weight over the last two months. It might be down to the takeaways I've been eating but I feel bloated. Zoe probably hasn't eaten a take-out meal all her life, and in my own way, I'm abusing her body. She didn't seem to notice, so I can't have put on that much weight. She probably wouldn't care anyway, as she made it quite clear that she's happy with changing my body to suit her new life.

Also, what exactly did she mean by '*Time's ticking*'? Does she mean the longer I take to try and reclaim my life, the less likely it will be that I can? She'll have gotten her claws into Luke far too deeply for me to prove my existence to him. It's like a game to her, she knows she holds all the cards and is trying to lure me into her game of chase. Well, I won't let her succeed. I can't let her succeed.

It's ten o'clock on Monday morning and I'm meeting up with Tom in an hour's time. Thank goodness we're only having a coffee. I think again how awkward it would be if we were eating out. Tom is a decent man, and good-looking. I can see that, anyone could. Zoe was lucky to have found a man like him. I felt defensive on his behalf when she described him as boring yesterday. I haven't found him boring as such, just difficult to get to know. Especially when he thinks you know him well enough to marry him already.

The plan is that I will get myself ready, meet with Tom at the time agreed and leave as soon as I can. That way I will have kept my promise but won't have to make idle chit-chat for too long. He has something important to tell me. I start to wonder what it could be.

Oh my goodness, I've just thought of something. He wants a divorce. I'm not sure how I feel about this. If he does want to divorce me, it would mean I am free from the guilt I feel every time I see him, but it will also mean I will then really be on my own. He's the only person who actually speaks to me. He doesn't know me, but he thinks he does.

Perhaps it wouldn't be a bad thing to split up with him. I have never been a complete believer in divorce. The vows you make during your marriage ceremony should be kept no matter what. But sometimes things don't work out as planned, and it's kinder on the two individuals to separate. If I were free from Tom, it would mean that I have to follow my path alone. I would have to be strong and I'd be able to find myself once again.

The time is now ten-thirty. My hair is nicely straightened. I've made an effort and put a little bit of make-up on and have dressed myself in skinny jeans and a floral knitted dress. It's important I make an effort today. I want to show Tom that I am getting better without his help. That way when he tells me he wants a divorce there will be no need for him to feel guilty.

My daily taxi arrives, but thankfully today it's a different driver.

Tom is sat in Bumbles already. He's obviously keen to meet up as I purposely arrived ten minutes early, hoping to be there before him. He must have arrived incredibly early as he is already halfway through a cappuccino.

'Morning Tom,' I say as I walk up to his table.

He gets up from his seat and moves round to pull my chair out for me. 'Hi Zoe, thanks so much for coming.'

He seems very formal today. I don't think I've ever had my chair pulled out by a man before. It makes me feel very special.

'That's OK, how are you?' I say.

'I'm OK, you look really good!' He seems to genuinely mean that, as his eyes widened when I greeted him.

He hands me a bundle of letters. 'These are for you, I don't know if any of them are important,' he says.

I take them from him. There are five letters in total, four of which look like standard bills. The other letter is written in script handwriting, addressed to me. I'll open them later at the B&B.

'I'll just go and order myself a coffee if that's alright?' I need to get away for a second to gather myself. I was hoping I'd have ten minutes when I arrived to do that, but he was too early a bird.

'No, no don't worry about that, I'll go and grab you one. What'll it be? Green tea as normal?' He asks.

I scoff. Now that's something I don't think I've ever ordered before, a green tea. Normally, it would be a hot chocolate with enough whipped cream to instantly clog my arteries.

'Actually, I quite fancy a hot chocolate please,' I say. 'I've been having more of an appetite for sweet and stodgy foods lately.'

Tom frowns. He looks confused. I guess anyone who knows Zoey would be confused by that request. She would be highly unlikely to ask for anything unhealthy.

'Whatever you want Zoe, you can have. It's always been that way, you know that.' Off he goes to go and get my drink.

Gino's is somewhere I used to come with Luke. It's the place to be in Taunton if you want a good drink, a nice chat and comfortable seats to relax on. If we were in town shopping, this is where we'd come when our legs were aching, and we couldn't carry any more shopping bags. Luke would have a Frappuccino and I would enjoy my coco treat.

Tom comes over carrying the largest hot chocolate they make. It's got their speciality whipped cream and chocolate flake on top. Delicious! He's obviously trying to butter me up before breaking the news to me.

'So … what was so important that you needed to talk to me face to face,' I ask him.

Tom shuffles in his chair, I can see his discomfort and it rubs off on me.

'Let's just enjoy our drinks first, shall we?' He says. 'So, what have you been up to since you left me?'

'I didn't leave you Tom, I just needed a break to get to know myself a bit better,' I say. 'I haven't really been doing much. I borrowed a laptop, so I've been on Facebook. I also researched the accident a bit.'

'Zoe, I thought I told you not to read up on the accident, it would only upset you.' He looks annoyed.

'Well, that's my choice isn't it? If I want to find out about what happened, then that's up to me.' His annoyance has pissed me off. 'Besides, I'm going to be making a lot more choices on my own from now on, aren't I? When you've told me what it is you need to say.'

'What are you talking about?' He asks. 'I'm not happy that you've been researching the accident, because I worry about you. I want you to make your own decisions, I always have. You're independent Zoe, and I wouldn't have you any other way.'

So, my independence is important to me and clearly to him. 'Just get on with it.'

'I'm sorry. I didn't come here for an argument. I'm not a mind reader so what is it that you think I'm going to tell you?'

'Look,' I start. 'It's clear that you're getting fed up with me. I would if I were in your shoes. I'll make it easy for you. I'm not sure how I feel about it, but if you want a divorce, I will give you one.'

Tom laughs. How dare he find this situation funny? The only person I can speak to wants to desert me and he finds it highly amusing.

'You think I want to divorce you?' He keeps laughing. 'Oh Zoe, I made those vows to you on our wedding day and meant every word. I don't want a divorce.'

Oh. 'Well, what is it then?'

'OK,' he says.' I know this isn't something you're going to want to hear. Your life has changed so much already, I worry that more change is going to be too hard for you. But the more time goes on, the sooner you need to know.'

'Please Tom, just spit it out.' I can't bear him dragging this out any longer. He needs to just tell me. I'm stronger now, and I can take whatever he tells me.

He pauses and composes himself. 'Zoe, you're pregnant.'

L. A. Evans

Part 3

17

My eyes remain focused on Tom's and I lower my hand to rest on my bloated abdomen. I'm pregnant. I'm having a baby. This can't be true. All my dreams of having my own child have come true.

Holding Tom's gaze, I say, 'You mean ...'

Tom interrupts, 'I'm sorry I didn't tell you sooner. We found out just before the accident. When you woke and I saw you were so confused, I didn't say anything. You didn't ask about the baby, so I put two and two together and figured you'd forgotten. Since then, I didn't know how to tell you. I'm sorry Zoe.'

So, I'm over two months gone. No wonder I've been feeling sick and bloated. I knew I was putting on weight, but I also knew I was eating more junk over the last two months than Zoe would have eaten in her lifetime. It would never have crossed my mind that I could be pregnant though. As far as I'm concerned, I can't have children. But Zoe could.

'*We* found out just before the accident?' I suddenly realised what he said. Zoe knew. Has she forgotten?

'Yes,' Tom says. 'It was a shock, to put it mildly. I was happy though, and I'll support you. You know I will.'

This is overwhelming. I have a child growing inside me. I will be a mother, but when? If Zoe knew before the accident, I must be due at the latest, March time. Judging by the size of my bloat, I can't be far gone.

'When is it due Tom?' I ask.

'We were given the due date of March the third,' he says.

My calculations were right. 'I *was* a month pregnant when I crashed. Were there any complications? The accident didn't cause any damage, did it?'

'We were so lucky Zoe,' he says. 'You were in such a critical condition. It was the worst time of my life.'

His voice starts to crack a little as the tears well in his eyes.

'Because your damage was to your head, they were concerned. They took you into surgery and ... well there were some complications. You had a cardiac arrest. They brought you back so quickly that there was no damage to the baby. But it was close Zoe. I almost lost the both of you. They did scans and tests, everything looked OK ...' He pauses. 'But we do have to go for a scan next week.'

Oh, my goodness. I died but was brought back. I think back to Zoe's blog, 'Reborn', she says there how she had to be resuscitated. She knew what her body had gone through on the operating table. How did she know? Did she remember? You hear stories of people seeing a white light as their soul leaves their body.

Now we must go to a scan. Fourteen weeks. That seems like ages when I think of everything that happened. But, in terms of pregnancy, it's very early stages. What if the scan finds something horrible because I haven't been looking after myself? What if there was damage from the accident? I certainly haven't been looking after myself since the accident.

I've been under a lot of strain and stress; the baby would have been through that too. I haven't been thinking of anyone other than myself. Well, from now on, there's someone else to think about.

I can't quite take all of this in. I've had enough surprises over the last couple of months, Tom was right. No wonder he didn't want to tell me. This is everything I've ever wanted. But with Luke. This child isn't Luke's, its Tom's. And it's not mine.

My bump contains the surrogate baby of Zoe and Tom Young. If I am to stay in this body, I will have to carry, give birth to and then raise someone else's baby. But it's a baby, and it's inside me!

This changes everything, or does it? For the past two months, all I've wanted is to return to my old life, my life with Luke, Gemma and my family. Now, with this revelation will I want to abandon this child? No, I want to carry, give birth to and raise it. Of course, I do. But it's not my child to keep.

Zoe must have forgotten she was pregnant. If she knew, I'm certain she would want her life back. There's no doubt about it. When she finds out, how will I feel? Split. She will want her life back. But will I?

'How do I feel about this Tom?' I ask. 'What is my reaction supposed to be? Have I always wanted a child? Did we plan a family?'

I have so many questions, most of which Tom wouldn't be able to answer.

Tom looks down at his hands, which rest on the table. 'I wanted a child, Zoe. But you didn't. Please listen to me when I say I will support you.'

I say nothing and wait for him to continue.

'You found out and hit the roof. We had an argument. I wanted it because I love you and want a child with you. You hated the idea of being a mother, of losing your figure and losing your career.'

He sighs. 'I have to be honest. I was toying with the idea of telling you. But I have to. You have the right to a choice, just as I do. You were going to get rid of it, Zoe.'

She was going to get rid of a child for no reason other than her selfishness. I feel sick. Zoe was blessed with the ability to fall pregnant. She had a loving husband who would support her and a healthy body to grow a child in. Yet, she had a choice, and she would choose to abort life's greatest miracle, a baby.

What do I do now? If I never return to my previous life, can I find the strength to do this? Even though Tom says he'll support me, he's saying he'll support Zoe, not me. I may have to face this on my own, but perhaps I'll want to.

*

The sun is shining behind the spire, silhouetting the church. The path winds through the familiar graveyard up to the main arched doorway. It's Monday afternoon and the church is open. I make my way inside.

I left Tom in the coffee shop. I couldn't talk about it anymore. I explained I needed to get this straight in my head and would speak to him soon. I told him not to worry because I wouldn't do anything without talking to him first. I wouldn't make any hasty decisions. How could I? Aborting Tom's child is not my decision to make.

The news that I am pregnant has completely thrown me. There is no-one I can talk to about it. The only place I can turn to is the church I know so well, the one I was christened in and later married in.

There are so many fond memories of this church. Every Sunday morning my parents would bring me here for the weekly service. My primary school held their Harvest and Christmas services here, in which I always played my part. But the best memory of all is my wedding day to Luke.

The sun's rays glow through the stained-glass windows casting a multitude of colours across the altar. I climb into the second pew and take a seat. I hear the bridal march playing through my head and feel the excitement and love of Luke on my special day. I can see Luke standing in front of where I'm sat, back turned, waiting for me to arrive by his side. I remember the vows we made to each other and how we meant them.

Churches have a particular smell. It's a mixture of wood, flowers and candles. I close my eyes, take in the scents surrounding me and pray. Every word I mean, emphasising them and believing they're being listened to. I ask God to give me the strength I need after receiving this news and help me make the right decision. I ask Him to look after my loved ones for me whilst I can't and find a way for them to come back to me. But if I never get my old life back, I ask that He helps me find a way through all this chaos and darkness to an even better life with those I hold dear by my side.

My head is bowed with my forehead resting on my clasped hands. There is the clunk of the wooden door latch and a creak as it opens. I finish my prayer with a desperate 'Amen' and turn around to see who it was that walked in.

I was expecting to see the vicar or churchwarden and was ready to make my excuses and leave. I didn't want people questioning why I was here. If I still looked like Aisha, they wouldn't bat an eyelid, but looking like Zoe, I was a stranger to them, and someone in need.

However, it wasn't the vicar or churchwarden, or anyone from the church committee. It was mum and dad.

I gasped, my jaw hitting the floor.

'What are *you* doing here?' My dad asked.

They recognise me from when I went to their house. 'I came here to pray,' I say. 'It's the only place I could think of to come. I feel safe here. I have so many happy memories of this place.'

My mum casts dad a sideways glance and says, 'We've never seen you here before.'

They wouldn't have. I don't think Zoe ever went to church. I doubt she'd ever set foot through the door of one.

I smile the kind that doesn't cause your eyes to smile with it. 'But you have, many times. You just don't see it.' I shake my head in sad frustration.

Mum and dad remain silent, they pass a few looks between them and walk towards my pew. They both take their seats next to me and bow their heads in prayer.

My dad, next to me, raises his head back up first and stares at the altar ahead of him. He whispers in a monotone voice, so as not to disturb mum's prayers, 'How are we to believe you?'

'That's what I prayed for.' I reply. 'I prayed that you would believe me. I'm pregnant and I want you both to be part of my child's life. I want you to be part of my life. You were always there for me, throughout everything. I pray that you learn to love me as I am now.'

'But how could this have happened? It doesn't make sense.' Dad says. 'Carol and I spoke about this after you left the other day. It's impossible. But something … something tells us it could be true.'

'That's because it is, dad. It is true.'

He stops talking, lowers his head again and closes his eyes.

*

The fresh air hits me outside in the churchyard. I left mum and dad in the church. I can't force them to believe me, but I hope and pray that they realise who I am.

There was not much more conversation. I tried to reminisce about my wedding day and dad walking me down the aisle. There was a brief mention of the Blu-Tack dad stuck on the bottom of my wedding shoe, and at that point I saw a slight twinkle of realisation cross my dad's face. But it soon faded.

I tried to talk to mum about granddad and the games we used to play. I tried to remind them how much we all missed him after he passed. But my tone was nonchalant. If they didn't believe me now, they never would. How could they ever believe me when I look like this?

My parents didn't say anything in response to my revelations. They kept quiet and occasionally looked at each other with sadness in their eyes. It was as if they wanted to believe me but didn't know how.

And now here I am, once again, on my own in the big wide world. But I'm not on my own, I have Bump to think about. The realisation hits me, and I know what I must do. I rub my belly and tell Bump, 'If your real mother doesn't want to know, then I will look after you. I will raise you as my own and love you until the day I die.'

I vow that I will always know my child and believe and trust in everything they say. No matter how impossible.

18

A week has passed since I visited the church. Most of my time was spent at the B&B watching TV, eating and sleeping. There was an occasional trip to the shop but apart from that I rested. It was important to rest as much as possible in anticipation of my looming scan.

I'd spoken to Tom two days ago and he told me our scan was scheduled for today, Monday morning, at ten o'clock. He was due to arrive in fifteen minutes giving us half-an-hour to get to the hospital.

Since our phone call two days ago, I've been constantly thinking about the scan. I've heard that you can sometimes find out the sex of the baby as early as thirteen weeks but I'm undecided if I want to know or not. I will leave that decision to Tom as it's not my place to decide.

My morning cup of de-caff coffee is too hot to drink and tastes like mud. As I tip the rest of it away in the bathroom sink, the phone in my room rings. It's Arthur telling me a man's asking for me, going by the name of Tom.

He's early. I tell Arthur I'll be down in a minute and ask that Tom wait downstairs. I'm not inviting him up here. This is my space and I'm not ready just yet to invite Tom into it.

My hair has grown enough now to scrape back into a ponytail, and I apply a little concealer and eye make-up before making my way downstairs.

Arthur stands behind his desk and greets me quizzically. He's obviously wondering who this strange man is as I've never mentioned a husband to him. I smile at him and nod, reassuringly. Arthur's been so good to me since I've been staying at his B&B. He's become a father figure. He always looks out for me and makes sure I'm safe and comfortable. But I keep my life private from him. It would confuse him too much if I started telling him what I've been through.

'Morning,' Tom beams. 'You ready?'

'As I'll ever be,' I smile back.

The conversation continues in his car on our way to hospital.

'So then,' he starts. 'If it's possible, are we finding out if we're having a baby boy or girl today?'

'I've decided that's up to you Tom. I've only just found out, whereas you've known all along. I think it's your decision.'

'Oh,' he says. 'Well, I think it's a joint decision. I mean, I'd like it to be a surprise, but if you want to know then that's OK with me.'

'To be honest, I don't mind. If it's not too early and we can find out if Bump's a boy or a girl, I'd be happy to know. If you want to keep it a surprise, I'll go with your decision.'

'Bump?' He looks surprised at my name for the baby. 'That's cute!'

'Well, it's better than saying he, she or it every time.'

'I'm just so pleased you're OK with all of this,' he says.

He seems so happy. When we talked on the phone, I agreed that we would keep Bump. How could I get rid of a living baby? It would go against all my morals and beliefs and it would be selfish. Bump deserves to be happy and loved, and I believe we can give that. Tom will be a fantastic father. From what I know of Tom, he will do anything for the ones he loves, and a parent's love for a child is unconditional. Tom's love for Zoe has been unconditional, so I know he will show Bump the same devotion.

'Right, so what exactly happens during this scan then?' I ask.

'Well, they check everything's OK, check the due-date is what we are expecting and the baby's size. If they can see the sex, they can tell us - if we want. I think that's mostly it,' he says. 'But the main thing is that we get to see Bump.'

I hadn't thought of this. So far, this pregnancy has felt like a dream. Today it will become a reality. I feel butterflies start to swarm in my belly.

'How big do you think Bump is?' I ask Tom.

'Well, I had a look on Google last night, and it should be about eight centimetres by now, about the size of a lemon.'

That's big. I thought it would be the size of a grape or at a push a plum. But a lemon means it's a fully formed mini baby.

*

'Please take a seat,' the sonographer says to me, ushering me to the bed. 'I expect you're looking forward to this. I'll be putting some gel on your abdomen which will feel quite cold, but it won't cause you any discomfort.'

I get comfortable and Tom stands by my side. After rolling my T-shirt up, the sonographer smears cold gel over my belly.

There is a muffled sound which changes into a quick pulsating noise. It's Bump's heartbeat.

Looking over to the computer screen, I can see a grainy picture of cloudy murk. Then, it comes into focus. Bump is curled on its back in the foetal position with what looks like a hand over their eyes.

I gasp and look over at Tom with a beaming smile and he grins back. I don't think about it but grab Tom's hand and squeeze it.

'There's Bump,' I say.

Our bump is a living thing, growing inside me. The reality hits and I am filled with overwhelming love and excitement. This is what it's like; this is what I've envied about every pregnant woman I've met. And now I get the chance to see my own baby, inside me.

Then it hits me. Reality once more bites down hard on my happiness. But it's not my baby. It's Tom's and Zoe's. I'm not here with Luke. This isn't my lifelong dream coming true. I remove my hand from Tom's and look away from the screen.

'Is everything OK?' Tom looks puzzled as he asks me. 'You all right?'

I take a deep breath. Grow a pair, I think to myself. This baby is growing inside me, I need to take responsibility. So, what if it's not mine? I have a duty to make sure it's healthy and I need to make sure it feels loved from day one. I give in to the situation.

The sonographer suddenly moves closer to the screen and turns it round to face him, and only him.

What's wrong? There's something wrong. It's my fault, I haven't looked after my body and now Bump has suffered. Tell us what's happened.

There's a cough, and a smile starts to appear across the sonographer's face. 'My apologies, Mr and Mrs Young, there was some confusion but it's nothing to worry about. It appears we have two heartbeats beating simultaneously.'

'Two?' Tom looks amazed. 'You mean … we're expecting twins?'

My eyes pop out of my head. I hadn't even gotten used to the idea of one child, let alone two. My mouth and throat have gone dry, but I manage to croak, 'Twins?'

'That's correct. I can confirm you have two of these little ones. Congratulations, it's a ready-made family,' the sonographer smiles.

*

Tom and I return to the car in shocked silence. This was not what we were expecting.

We found out that the twins were indeed due on March the third. That date didn't change. They were healthy and they each had all twenty digits in the right place. The sonographer couldn't tell us the sexes even if we wanted to know. But we were told we could find out at 20 weeks if we wanted. The main thing today is that our babies are healthy, and the accident didn't cause any noticeable damage.

We've signed up to an antenatal care regime. Now that we're expecting twins, it's important to be seen on a regular basis. I was advised to eat healthily, but there's no need to eat more than normal just because I'm carrying two.

The sonographer was correct, it was a ready-made family. This is the first time, since the accident, I feel that I fit in the world. I have a purpose in life, and that is to ensure the safe arrival of these two little mites and raise them as my own. I have a family. And I know I want it.

19

My room at the B&B is as it was when I first arrived. I take a moment to look around one final time, grab my bags and head downstairs. Arthur is at his desk as normal and clocks me as I descend the final steps.

'Time for me to check out, Arthur,' I say.

For a couple of seconds, disappointment spreads across Arthur's face, then it slowly disperses, and a loving smile takes its place.

'It's been an absolute pleasure, my dear,' he replies.

I owe Arthur so much. Although he doesn't know much about what's happened to me, he's been so supportive and caring. It's been good in a way that he hasn't known my business as it's meant I've been able to keep my bubble of my B&B room separate from the confusion of my world outside.

'I don't know how to repay you,' I say. 'You've been so … great! Thank you so much, for everything.'

'No need for thank yous,' he says. 'Just know where I am, whenever you need me, anything at all now.'

'Thank you, Arthur.'

Tom appears at the B&B entrance and takes my bags from me. I cast Arthur one final smile, blow him a kiss and follow Tom out to the car.

Since finding out I am carrying twins, I have gained a new perspective. I'm not leaving my old life behind. My past with Luke will always be a part of me. However, I have to look to the future. If that means a future with Tom and our children, then so be it. I must stop dwelling in the past and move on. I feel as though I have been in limbo for too long now. Constantly thinking of what I had and what I could have had, rather than what I have now and what I will have in the future.

In the car, I sit and watch Tom as he drives and talks. He is so happy to be bringing me home. I'm not really paying much attention to what he is saying, but merely nodding and smiling every now and then when he turns to me for a response. I have no strong emotions. There's no sadness, happiness or excitement, I just feel, content.

Pulling up the drive, the house looks every bit as impressive as I remember it. My mind was not in the right frame last time I stayed here. Now, I start to feel a little bit excited. This is going to be my new life. I'm with a man who clearly adores me and we're going to be having a family. It's not what I planned, but then nothing really happens in life as you expect it to. Everything happens for a reason, it's time to find out what that reason is.

*

Tom has been cleaning. The house is spotless and there's a beautiful flower arrangement waiting for me in the kitchen. And, even better, there are no lilies.

'I've got your bed ready for you in your bedroom. I'll be in the spare room but not far away if you need anything. Would you like me to take your bags up now?' Tom asks.

'No, no. That's OK. Thanks Tom.'

The bedroom is bright and airy; the window's open letting in a cool October breeze. Tom's left me to unpack whilst he's gone to get us pizza for tea. I've asked for pepperoni, which caused some concern for him. But I quickly explained that the pregnancy's given me the taste for meat again, which he thankfully believed.

There's not much to unpack but it takes me a very long time. For every piece of clothing I put away in the wardrobe, I take another out for the charity shop. If I'm going to start again here, I need to get rid of Zoe's clothes.

Before I know it, I've bagged up three bin liners full of clothes to take to the charity shop. And have decided tomorrow's task is to go maternity clothes shopping. I'm going to be getting bigger and the clothes I have remaining won't stay comfortable for long. It's time to get rid of the old stuff and bring in the new.

My bags are empty apart from the side zip. As I open the zip, I see the post Tom gave me, still unopened.

Sure enough, as I expected there were bills and club card vouchers. But there was still the one written by hand to open. For a moment, guilt rears its ugly head, and I don't feel as though I should be opening something personal addressed to Zoe. But then again, she didn't hesitate to open my personal letter from the doctors. So, I tear it open.

Dear Zoe,

I'm so sorry to hear about your accident and I'm sorry I didn't visit. I've tried to write so many times, but I keep binning them because I just don't know what to say.

We haven't spoken for so long, and even though you really hurt me, I need to know you're OK. Please don't be angry, but I have spoken to Tom and he told me all about your accident and your coma.

There are some things that have been playing on my mind about the day of your accident which I need to talk to you about. I need to know what you decided to do. I don't want another row. I just want to talk to you.

I forgive you for what you did. It has taken time, but I just want my sister back. Please write back or phone me on my mobile. It really would be lovely to hear from you.

Lots of love as always,

Melanie x

I have a sister! Well, Zoe has a sister. She said she didn't have any family, but here, in writing it says she has a sister. What is she forgiving Zoe for? What did Zoe do? It sounds pretty bad if they haven't spoken for ages. I wonder what Melanie's like and if she looks like me.

Tom told me I was an only child. How dare he lie? What else has he lied about?

This is yet another revelation which has started questions in my mind again. I may have lost my best friend, but it's possible I've just gained a sister and I want to know everything about her. I can't believe he kept this from me.

I need to contact her. Excitedly I start rummaging around for some writing paper and a pen but stop. How do I explain that I know nothing about Melanie? Can I go through this again? Having to explain myself, lie and make excuses? Not only that but put someone else through it after what I put Tom through. I think it is best I talk to Tom first about this. He told me I was an only child. Perhaps he did that for a reason, to protect me from something. Zoe and Melanie obviously had a big argument, which I know nothing about. I need to tread carefully.

*

When Tom arrives home with pizza, it's clear something's playing on my mind and he's instantly aware of my mood.

Putting the pizzas down on the kitchen table, Tom asks me what's happened. He's worried it's something he's done so I reassure him he's done nothing, tell him to start eating whilst it's hot and begin to explain.

'Tom, I opened a letter this afternoon from the pile you gave me. It was from Melanie.'

He's about to bite into his first piece of pizza and freezes then places it back in the box.

'I'm so sorry,' he says. 'I should have told you, but I have my reasons. What did it say, if you don't mind me asking?' He says.

I read the letter out to him.

'Yes, you should have told me,' I say. 'I feel really bad that I don't know my own sister. She obviously wants to make contact, but I know what I put you through and I really don't want to do the same thing to a sister I don't remember. Why didn't you tell me?'

I continue. 'You know how important it is to me to know about my past. If I stand any chance of looking to the future, you can't keep things like this from me. It's clear we had a big argument at some point, which again I know nothing about. I don't know what to do. I feel stronger but, I don't know if I'll be opening a can of worms or not. Please, tell me everything now, and be honest.'

Tom lowers his head so that I can't see his face. When he raises it again, I can see tears in his eyes.

'It was a while ago now Zoe,' he starts. 'It's my fault. I wasn't giving you enough attention and you were bored. I suggested we started socialising more and invited Mel and Steve, her husband, around more often.'

He clears his throat and continues. 'We invited them to barbeque afternoons and they invited us out for meals. It was lovely, doing things as couples and I thought it was bringing us closer together as well. But it wasn't.'

'Mel returned from work one day to find you and Steve...' Tom breaks and I grab his arm in a vain attempt to comfort him.

'Go on,' I encourage him, gently squeezing his arm. I can see it's difficult for him to tell me, but I need to know.

'You'd been having an affair with Steve for three months, we found out. Six months ago, Mel separated from Steve and decided to move to New Zealand. She cut all contact with you. That's why I didn't tell you. I wanted to protect your feelings.'

That little bitch. The more I find out about Zoe, the more I despise her. How could she do that to Tom and to her sister?

'What about you? You forgave me?' I ask.

He swallows and takes both my hands. 'Of course, I did. You were so apologetic, and I love you. We're married, and I wanted to make this work. Don't get me wrong, it was hard and there were images in my head that were hard to erase. But over time they faded. I promised you then that things would be different. I'd pay you my full attention and love you the way you deserved to be loved.'

'It wasn't your fault. I must have been incredibly selfish and cruel to make you think you caused me to have an affair. I'm the one who did it. I'm sorry.'

Genuinely I feel awful. I know it wasn't me who did this to him, it was her, Zoe. But I feel responsible because he believes I am her.

'Let's not go over this again,' Tom says. 'There's no need to apologise, you were sorry enough back then. We were both in the wrong, but we worked through it. I forgave you and you forgave me. And now, well now we have two little lives to think of. I'm sorry I lied.'

I can see he genuinely means it. 'Please just be honest with me in future OK?'

Something inside me that's been bubbling away for the last few minutes rises to the surface and I hug Tom. I squeeze him so hard. He's finally opened up to me and I feel closer to him than ever before. There's a need inside me to protect him. Protect Tom from getting hurt again, protect him from Zoe.

Before I know it, I say, 'Don't sleep in the spare room tonight. You can stay with me. If you want?'

Let's start as we mean to go on. We're married and expecting twins. If I'm going to play happy families, I ought to share a bed with my husband.

'Really?' Tom stutters. 'You mean … Don't feel you have to … if it's too soon? I'll understand.'

'No time like the present,' I say. 'I'm back, and I'm here to stay. Thank you for being patient. There will still be times when I need my own space and I know you'll acknowledge that, but we're married. I need to start being a wife again.'

Tom doesn't say anything, he doesn't need to. It's written all over his face. A warm feeling settles in the pit of my stomach because I know I've made him so happy. If I can make him happy, I believe it will in time, make me happy too.

20

Last night I spent with Tom hugging me to sleep. It felt surprisingly welcome. After our conversation around Zoe's affair with Steve I realised my growing affection for Tom. It's clear he dotes on me and loves me unconditionally even after my doing something so unspeakable to hurt him.

I've always had the opinion that if someone in a relationship is tempted to stray, instead of following that instinct and not giving a second thought to their partner, they should re-evaluate their relationship and consider what it is that is tempting them to have an affair. There must be something wrong with their relationship. Therefore, they have two options, either they work things out with their partner, or they break up. An affair should never be an option.

Zoe clearly didn't share the same opinion. She obviously didn't give a toss about Tom or his feelings but cared solely about herself. Likewise, she didn't care about hurting her sister or losing her.

As someone who has longed for a sibling, in particular a sister, I find it incredibly difficult to contemplate doing something like that to them. Gemma was the closest thing I had to a sister and to hurt her like that would be unthinkable. Sisters share so many memories, there must have been so many good times spent between Mel and Zoe which were discarded when Zoe had an affair with Steve.

Don't get me wrong, it takes two to tango, so Steve was as much in the wrong. However, to hurt not only your husband but also flesh and blood is something I struggle to understand.

I think back to my marriage to Luke, and question what I would do if he had an affair. Would I be as forgiving as Tom? Probably not, but until you're in that situation you don't know what you would do.

It shows such strength in Tom's character. Many people would see it as a weakness, taking someone back after they betrayed you. I see him as a man who stands by his marriage vows. A man who believes in the sanctity of marriage and a man who loves, understands and forgives. It takes a certain kind of person to summon the strength to forgive.

Even though it wasn't me who cheated on Tom, I feel I owe him. He took Zoe back, and I must do the same.

I touch my bump and think of the little mites entering this world and how I can now protect them from their mother. Could what happened to me be for this reason? For them to receive the maternal love they deserve and the security of married parents.

And then it dawns on me. Are the twins definitely Tom's? Has he asked the same question, or does he know they are for certain?

What a mess these children could have been born into.

*

At breakfast I decide to ask Tom his opinion. I've been thinking about it all day, wondering if he's prepared to possibly bring up someone else's children. Maybe he believes they are his and I'm going to be playing devil's advocate to the detriment of his feelings. Either way, I can't bring up these children knowing that I am not their biological mother *and* wondering if he is their biological father.

'Can I ask you something please, Tom?'

'Of course, you can,' he replies.

'There's been something playing on my mind since we talked last night but I don't want to upset you.'

He looks at me reassuringly, so I proceed.

I take a deep breath. 'Do you think the twins are yours?'

Tom thinks for a while and says, 'I've asked myself the same question. But I believe they are, yes. It was six months ago that you had your affair and our relationship got so much better. Steve moved up north, so I know he's not around anymore.'

'But you told me I wanted an abortion. Don't you think this could be because they aren't yours?'

I've overstepped the mark. 'Sorry, but I worry. I don't want you to feel you have to bring up these children if there's any doubt in your mind that you're their father.'

'There will always be some doubt in my mind. You cheated on me once, who's to say you wouldn't again? But the day we found out you were expecting, I made a promise to my unborn child, to myself and to you. I promised I would be the best father I possibly could be.'

This is insane. How can he be so forgiving and have such compassion? I hear myself saying, 'You're amazing, do you know that?'

He smiles and gives a small snort.

'No seriously,' I say. 'You forgave me when I did the worst thing possible.'

I walk over to Tom and crouch down next to him with my hands on his knees and say, 'I will never cheat on you, ever again. I'm a different person now. In time, you will learn to trust me again. I will make sure of that.'

And I genuinely mean it.

*

The house phone is in my hand and I'm bracing myself ready to dial. I've written myself a script, so I know what to say and don't get tongue-tied. I press the buttons slowly then bring the phone to my ear.

There's a foreign ringtone unlike UK landlines. It rings three times, and a woman answers it.

'Hello?' She says.

I can hear a faint New Zealand twang to her vowels. My throat goes dry and I can't bring myself to read my pre-prepared script. I hang up.

This is ridiculous. Mel said in her letter that something has been playing on her mind about the day of the accident. She may have some answers for me, but I can't handle my nerves for long enough to even say hello.

If I ever want to move on with my life, I need to speak to her. I dial again.

'Hello?' She sounds a little more agitated this time.

'… Hello,' I manage.

'Oh my God,' she says. 'Zoe? It's you, isn't it?'

The script goes out of the window. 'Yes, it's me.'

The line goes quiet.

After a few seconds Mel says, 'I'm so pleased you rang. How are you?'

'I'm actually OK, thanks. It's been hard, but I'm getting there. Look, I need to be honest with you from word go. I don't remember anything before the accident.'

'Oh,' she says. 'So, you don't ...'

'... Tom told me everything. How I treated you, what I did to you both. It's awful and I'm so ashamed of myself. I'm so sorry.'

'As I said in my letter, I forgive you. It has taken me a while, but I do now.' Mel says. 'You really can't remember anything? What about Tom, do you remember him?'

'No, he's a stranger. However, I'm getting to know him now. What I'm about to say may upset you again, so I'm sorry in advance ... I'm sure we've got loads of memories of growing up, but I don't share them with you, anymore.' I say.

'It's a horrible situation, but it must be worse for you. There are loads of memories, but in time, hopefully you will gain some back. If not, we'll have to make some new ones. I'd like to say we always got on, but …' She gives an ironic giggle.

I can tell it's a nervous laugh, probably because she doesn't know what to say. I don't either.

I cut to the chase. 'Mel, I'm trying to piece together bits of information I'm learning about the accident and my life before. In your letter you said something had been playing on your mind about the accident. Can I ask what?'

She sighs. 'We don't need to talk about that now. I just want to know you're OK.'

There's something she's hiding from me and I need to know.

'Mel, we do need to talk about it. There's obviously something troubling you and I'm trying so hard to remember things. Anything you know could help me.'

'Did Tom tell you your … um … news?' Mel asks.

'News? Oh … do you mean the pregnancy?' I reply.

'I wasn't sure if you'd know yet.' She replies, a little hesitantly. 'How do you feel about it?'

I pause. 'Well, I'm not going to lie, it was a shock. But I'll tell you a bigger shock … we just went for my scan and we've found out we're having twins!'

The line goes silent again.

'Are you there, Mel?'

'Yes, I'm here! Sorry, it took a while to sink in there. Are you happy about this? I mean … I know you didn't want to keep … um …' she sounds concerned.

'I know,' I say. 'Tom told me I wanted an abortion.'

'So … you didn't get there in time?' She says.

Didn't get there in time? What does she mean by that?

'Sorry, what do you mean?' I ask.

She pauses. 'That's where you were going, when you had your accident. You were going to the clinic. Tom didn't know.'

Zoe was going to have an abortion without telling Tom. I don't know why I'm surprised. It's yet another thing Zoe was quite happy to do when others wouldn't dream of it.

Mel can tell this is news to me as I've gone quiet. She adds, 'I'm sorry. I would have thought you'd have remembered that. That's what I meant, in my letter. I needed to know if you'd gone through with it or not. Obviously, you didn't, but not through choice.'

'How do you know this? I thought we hadn't spoken for months?'

'I contacted you when I found out you were pregnant. I wanted to try to rebuild our relationship.' Mel says. 'But when you told me you were going to have an abortion without telling Tom, I just couldn't agree. We had another row about it and then … then you had your car crash.'

I completely see where Mel is coming from. She seems to have the same morals as me, but not as Zoe. I need her to realise that I would never hurt these children and will raise them and love them.

'Since finding out I was pregnant, after my accident, I've been so happy. I want you to know I want these twins so much. I promise I will be the best mother I can be.'

There is a faint sound of sobs, Mel's started crying.

'I'm so pleased,' she manages to say. 'I needed to know you were happy with your pregnancy. I just don't understand why you feel so differently now.'

She's right not to understand. I am so different from Zoe yet appear to be the same person. It's hard to try to convince someone I am a completely different person. I don't want to keep lying to Mel, but at the same time, I can't face trying to explain to her what happened to me, for fear of yet another person thinking I'm crazy.

I try to explain cautiously. 'I'm not the same person I was. I can't go into detail at the moment but believe me when I say the accident changed me. I may look the same from the outside, but I'm completely different inside.'

I continue. 'I don't expect you to understand, I just hope one day you will see it for yourself.'

'I really hope so, Zoe,' Mel says, through lessening sobs. 'When Tom told me that you had to be resuscitated, I was so worried about you. You died Zoe. At 3.15pm your heart stopped beating and I was fast asleep in my own New Zealand world none the wiser. I never want to be so far away from you again.'

'Well, you are currently the other side of the world,' I say. 'But I'll always be at the end of the phone.'

Mel goes quiet again for a few seconds and then says, 'I'm actually at the airport. I'm ready to come home. My plane departs to the UK in thirty minutes. I hope you'll come and meet me?'

A mixture of dread and excitement overwhelms me.

21

My mind is again a whirlwind of emotion. I've just found out I'm expecting twins, moved back in with my 'new' husband, have just decided to give my new life a go, and now I'm on my way to Bristol airport to meet a sister I've only just found out about.

Mel's flight arrives at ten-past-ten this morning and Tom and I are in arrivals waiting to meet her. Thankfully it's a Sunday, so Tom could come with me.

The car journey to the airport was relaxed and felt natural. We talked about Tom's work, the customers and the people he works with. He had a few groans about Clive, a colleague, who's lazy and does nothing to help. He told me everyone keeps asking after me and wondering when I'll be coming back to work. Karen misses me and wants me to come back.

The name Karen rang a bell, and it took a while for me to register who Tom was talking about. She was the one I bumped into shortly after moving into the B&B. She must think I've lost my marbles, but then again.

We discussed the prospect of my return to work. I've never been to a gym let alone worked in one, so I explained it would be too hard to adjust back to a job I'd done before the accident. People would be asking too much about it, and it would just feel awkward. I explained I'd be better off starting afresh in a new career. Tom agreed, thankfully.

I told Tom I'd been thinking about setting up my own business. Possibly charity based for children with disabilities, it would be a club for them to get into sports and meet like-minded children. That way it incorporated my love of helping others and Zoe's fitness career.

At first, I don't think Tom really believed me. I mean, Zoe isn't the kind of person who would naturally be interested in charity work or helping others. But I explained the accident opened my eyes a little to the world. I was given a second chance, and I want to use the rest of my life in a positive light. He seemed to understand and said we could research it and he'd support my decision.

Financially we wouldn't benefit. However, we have no mortgage and no other major outgoings. Tom brings home some income but the interest on our investments will keep us afloat of our bills and lifestyle. He'd always said he only worked at the gym for the social aspect rather than the take-home.

Personally, I feel I need to be doing something with my life. I need to move on, look to the future and this would be something of mine, a new beginning.

Waiting in arrivals I'm starting to get anxious. This is Zoe's sister, and she knows Zoe inside out. She's bound to think I'm someone I'm not, so it'll take some work on my part to convince her I've changed.

The ten-year-old Aisha inside me is getting excited at the prospect of gaining a sister. I try and push her to the back of my mind and concentrate on the facts. This is Zoe's sister, not mine. Mel is a stranger to me; someone I need to get to know. But not just need to, want to.

People of all ages start emerging from the gateway. Families of three, four and five people struggle with their huge, bulging suitcases. A man in a suit rushes through the crowd with his leather case trailing behind him and his mobile perched on his shoulder. On the other side of the gateway, family members and loved ones greet the passengers with kisses and hugs, and business folk meet with their drivers.

Tom nudges my arm and says, 'There she is.'

I peer through the crowds wondering who he's referring to. And then my eyes are drawn to a girl of same height and same facial structure as me but with short, red, spiky hair. I feel my hair prickle on my skin. That must be Mel.

She quickens her pace lifting her suitcase up for more speed.

'Zoe!' She beams, running up to me. She discards her suitcase and flings her arms around me. 'I'm so pleased you're OK. Thanks so much for coming to meet me.'

With both hands on my shoulders, she casts her head back slightly to take in my face. I don't really know what to do, so I grin impishly at her.

'And hello you,' she moves her attention over to Tom and plants a smacker on his cheek.

'Oh, I've missed you guys so much,' Mel says. 'It feels so good to be home, I can't tell you how much!'

From first impressions Mel is like a bumblebee. Beautiful, slightly irritating but you instantly want to protect her. The way she carries herself is so confident. Dramatic make-up is drawn all around her green eyes and her clothes are uniquely bright and over-the-top. She's younger than me, you can tell through her mannerisms and vibrancy.

'Man, have we got so much to catch up on!' she says.

For someone whose heart was broken by me, she seems so carefree and loving towards me. It instantly relaxes me so I flatten my bristles and can't help but smile. Tom takes her suitcase and Mel squeezes between me and Tom, links arms with us both and walks us back to the car.

*

Over the next few weeks, Mel and I grew closer together. She stayed with us for a couple of weeks before moving into a flat a couple of miles away. She reminds me so much of Gemma. She has such a positive outlook on the world that it's so refreshing to be around her. We've cleared the air and she's been so gracious in forgiveness towards me.

She's told me so many tales about her time in New Zealand, the men she's dated, the places she's been and the places she's worked. Mel's a beauty therapist. She had a business in the UK called *Beaut*. She sold the premises while she was in New Zealand and tried to start the business again out there, but it didn't work out. But she's ready now to give it another go in the UK.

Whilst in New Zealand, Mel dated many men, slept around a bit, but she said it's something she needed to do. She was with Steve for almost fifteen years so had never been with any other men. Therefore, when Steve had an affair with Zoe, it hurt her immensely, but it meant she could find herself again.

We talked about my accident, my relationship with Tom and my ideas for the future. I felt I could open up to Mel in a way I haven't done with anyone since Gemma and Luke. I haven't told her what happened to me in entirety, but I explained how different I am now, and how my outlook on life has changed.

I could tell Mel was surprised when she found out I no longer survived on veg alone and had found my appetite for takeaways and all non-healthy food. She'd assumed this was due to the twins, so I played along with it.

Mel really sang Tom's praises. It was clear that she thought very highly of him. Partly for the forgiveness he'd shown towards me but generally for the love and partnership he'd given me over the years. She described him as a 'good catch'. And I agreed.

There were times that Mel would talk about the past. She would tell me about our childhood and our parents. She told me about a game we used to play in the garden when one of us would be blindfolded and be given an object to identify. One time, Mel was blindfolded, and I placed a chicken-poo in her hands. Mel roared telling me I did this, claiming she still hadn't forgiven me for making her squeeze a warm, fresh chicken-poo in her hand. I laughed along with her memories, but it was clear I didn't share them.

I found out some interesting things about Zoe's parents. They were very well off and spoilt their children with gifts and material objects. However, they rarely showed affection. Their way of showing love was to buy their children an up-to-date Walkman or the first ever Gameboy.

Mel told me she thought I was their favourite which was hard to digest. The inheritance went solely to Zoe as the elder daughter. Zoe gave Mel enough to buy *Beaut* and kept the rest for herself. Mel wasn't bitter when she told me this. She explained that she told me – that is Zoe - to keep the rest. All she needed was enough to start her own business. I didn't believe her.

I decided then and there that if I were to remain as Zoe, I would repay her somehow for everything, one way or another.

*

For a November morning the sun is shining brightly and views from my bedroom window are as clear as on a summer's day. I've only just woken up after a terrible night's sleep. I haven't had nightmares for a few months now, but last night they returned.

Last night I dreamt of the junction again. This time I could hear the music being played from the radio and recall a couple of lines: *I've much on my mind and no way to turn, Should I go back or keep moving on?*

It was pouring down with rain. In the car with me were Tom and Mel and as I pulled up to the junction, Mel screamed, 'Zoe, stop!' I slammed my foot on the brakes as a man and woman slowly crossed the road in front of me. They both had hoods pulled up over their faces and walked with their heads down. Following them was a hearse. I looked in the rear-view mirror and saw a van approaching me and gaining speed. I braced myself for impact and the van crashed into the back of my car, spinning us around and around, faster and faster.

Once the car slowed down again, my eyes came back into focus. The funeral procession had vanished, and Tom and Mel were no longer in the car. They were replaced by two corpses, Luke and Gemma.

Tom has already left for work, not that I would tell him about this dream anyway. But it would have been comforting to have him here this morning.

Meeting Mel and building a relationship with both her and Tom has probably triggered this nightmare. The fact that I'm dreaming of the death of people in my life as Aisha can mean only one thing. It's time to move on. The lines from the song keep ringing through my head. I don't know what the song is but it's so clear now in my mind. Should I go back or keep moving on? My unconscious mind is telling me to leave the past behind me and concentrate on the present and my future with Tom and Mel. It's the only way to turn now.

Junction ~ Time's Ticking

22

My business idea has grown into fruition. Tom helped me develop my plans, he came with me to see a financial adviser and we looked at different premises. Mel also helped as she recently re-started *Beaut* in Taunton town centre, so she shared some business skills with me.

We found an ideal building on the outskirts of town which used to be an old community centre. It consists of a main hall and a playing field at the back. There was some work that needed doing to make it viable for disabled children, as an example the doors needed widening and ramps needed to be put in place. But after consulting some specialists and a lot of hard work and dedication, the business is now open. Taking both Tom's and my new surname into account, I've called it *Young Stars*.

260

It's a constant juggling act between getting sponsors and running it, but it gets me out of the house, and I am thoroughly enjoying putting in the hours. It only runs in the afternoons from three o'clock until seven o'clock, so it means the mornings are still my own. We also open from nine o'clock on Saturdays for three hours when Tom often comes to help.

Four volunteers have also joined me, so I know that the place will be well looked after when I become too tired to work as labour day approaches. It also means the business will still run after the birth, meaning I can take some maternity time off.

There are twelve children who regularly come each afternoon and I can see they really enjoy the interaction with me and the other children which leaves me feeling satisfied. The children play sports outside and inside, we hold cake and jumble sales to raise funds for the centre and do other educational and creative activities.

Today we are making Christmas cards. There's a new boy who joined a week ago, called Bobby. He's quite a quiet child, keeps himself to himself. He has learning difficulties but loves to do arts and crafts.

He's sat by himself with a pot of glitter, a bag of cotton wool and some PVA glue. He's managed to get more of the stuff on his hands and face than on the Christmas card but he's the happiest I've seen him.

'Hello Bobby,' I say. 'Ooo ... so who's this lovely card going to be for?'

There is so much concentration on Bobby's face that he can barely raise it to look at me. 'It's for my Uncle Dave and Auntie Carol. To say thank you.'

'Thank you for what Bobby?' I ask.

'They look after me while my mummy and daddy work sometimes. There're fetching me today and then taking me for food.'

'Well, I'm sure they'll love it,' I reply.

The parents often come into the hall to meet their children and stay for a tea or coffee. It's something I like to do to involve them. They never stay for long, but quite often long enough to sup a quick cuppa.

Today is no different. At six-forty-five they start to come in, chatting amongst themselves. At six-thirty I always ask the children to start packing away whilst I set up the table with tea and coffee cups, boil the kettle and fill the urn with help from my volunteers.

I'm taking a parent's coffee order when Bobby bounces over to me beaming with a cheeky grin, the kind that even the sourest of people can't avoid responding to with a smile of their own.

'Zoe!' He shrieks. 'This is Uncle Dave and Auntie Carol.'

Dave and Carol. Why didn't I twig before?

'We meet again,' my dad says, a kind smile forming across his face.

*

Parental love is unconditional. They love you no matter what you do, who you are or who you become.

I once read in one of my trashy magazines about a mother whose son tried to kill himself and his family. He drugged his wife and two children, put them all in their beds and set the house on fire. No-one died, but he was arrested, taken to court and sent down for eighteen years. Yet, his mother visited him in prison every week and told the reader how she loved him even though he committed this terrible crime.

The son blamed his behaviour on his upbringing. He was raised by an abusive stepfather and told the court that it was because of him that he was damaged. Excessive alcohol consumption also played a part.

You may wonder how and why this could have happened to the wife and children. If there is justice or divine intervention in this world, why could this happen? Later on, in the story, the mother tells how the wife and children now live abroad with another father-figure and are the happiest they have ever been.

The mother's story showed great sympathy towards her son and pleaded awareness of abusive upbringings and the damage they can cause in later life. She showed no regret or hatred towards her son. If anything, she stated that these things happen, and they happen for a reason. And the reason in the case of this story is so that her son receives the help he's needed since childhood and the rest of the family live a happy and fulfilling life.

Now, I haven't killed anyone. My fate was not self-inflicted. What happened to me after crashing my car was out of my control. Zoe and I switched places, for reasons unknown. However, I am starting to understand why this may have happened.

My life before the accident was enjoyable. It was secure, with Luke, Gemma and my parents. I liked my job as a care worker and I enjoyed my evenings in with Luke, watching the TV, curled up on the sofa. It was all I knew.

However, I couldn't have children, didn't have any close siblings and even though I liked my job as a care worker, I didn't love it.

Since becoming Zoe and stepping into her shoes, my eyes have been opened to many other possibilities. I still have a network of support, have recently grown closer to Tom than I ever imagined I would and have finally gained a sister who loves me unconditionally. I'm now leading my own business doing what I love the most. But ultimately, I am about to embark on motherhood, something that is so close to my heart.

Zoe has made it clear that she is happy living my life. Should I ever find a way back to my loved ones again, I would be ecstatic. I have finally realised that should I return; I would also be leaving behind so many new memories and would miss my life as Zoe terribly.

*

My parents are here, at *Young Stars*. I can't believe it! Although, they both seem to have a few more wrinkles and appear a little troubled.

'It's really nice to see you both again,' I say. 'I'm just making a cuppa for a mum, but I can make you both one too if you like?'

They bring Bobby over to the table and sit down with him whilst I make them both a brew.

I hand them over two mugs. 'There you go, one with some extra 'taste' and one with the tea bag left in. Just how you both like it.'

Mum gives my dad a baffled look and he glances back at her with a look that says *I told you so*. They didn't tell me how they liked their tea. They didn't need to.

My dad takes a sip of tea and says, 'This your business then? It's got a good reputation already. Bobby certainly loves it here.'

'His parents live next door,' he continues. 'We've started helping them a bit, looking after Bobby, as they work so hard.'

The penny drops, I know Bobby. He's Sandra-from-next-door's son. I never knew his name.

'Oh of course,' I say. 'Sandra and Derek from next door, I never twigged. It is great *Young Stars* is getting a reputation already, it's not been set up long.'

I'm trying hard to make them realise it's me. Surely, they can't think it's still a coincidence that I know so much about them.

'We didn't congratulate you when we saw you at the church,' my mum says, looking at my bump. 'Not properly anyway, Dave told me you were expecting.'

'Oh … yes. It came as quite a shock,' I say.

'When is it due?'

'They're due in March,' I reply coyly.

'They?' My mum looks at my dad again but doesn't appear happy about the news. She tries to hide her sadness, but I can see it.

'Yes, I'm having twins, which came as an even bigger shock,' I say.

This time, I don't want to blow it. 'Look, I know you don't believe what I told you a couple of months ago. But I want you to know that I'm happy and that I'm safe. It's important that you know that.'

My dad nods with his lips curled ever so slightly at the corners. 'This isn't the place to talk. Perhaps you would like to pop round to ours some time?'

*

It's so comforting to be back in my parents' lounge. My heart is beating ten-to-the-dozen. My parents have invited me to theirs, to talk. I must control my emotions though. To them, I am still a stranger. Although, I can't help getting my hopes up just a little bit.

My mum has prepared afternoon tea with the best cutlery, comprising of sandwiches and cakes. She's prepared a guest-spread as I used to call it. It's when my mum goes over the top for visitors, trying to convince them we live like this all the time.

They've been very welcoming, but it feels a little tense and awkward. They're making such an effort to welcome me, but it feels forced. Hopefully when we're eating it'll be a bit more natural. My mum comes into the lounge with a pot of tea and ushers me to the dining table.

'Well … are you going to find out the sexes?' My mum asks as she pours.

'We've talked about it, as it would be easier to know, especially with having twins. But we've decided to keep it as a surprise.'

My dad clears this throat. 'Who's the father?'

'Dave!' My mum scowls at him across the table.

'What? I was just asking!' He claws back at her.

'It's OK,' I say. 'My husband is called Tom. Over the past few months, I've got to know him and he's a decent bloke. You'd both really like him.'

As we eat and drink, our conversations centre on *Young Stars* and general chit-chat.

I used to love family meals growing up. We would always eat at the table, my parents deemed it important to eat and talk about the day.

Sunday lunches were always the best. Mum would put the meat on to cook before we all headed out to church. By the time we were home, they just needed to put the veg on to boil and make the gravy. When we ate, we'd talk about all sorts of things. Quite often, Dad would talk about my ancestry, past aunts, uncles, great grandparents and even great-great-grandparents. I used to love hearing funny stories about relatives I never knew.

The conversation today is gradually starting to feel a bit more natural. My dad cracks jokes, my mum chides him, and I laugh. Dad has been telling me about a cat he had as a child that almost got cooked when it fell asleep in the oven. I've heard this story many times over the years, but it still makes me chuckle, knowing it survived its near roasting. Then the conversation turns.

My dad puts down his cutlery and says, 'You remember when you knocked on our door shortly after the accident? We told you Aisha had been acting differently.'

I nod and let him continue, I don't want to interrupt for fear of cutting him off. He seems to be leading somewhere with this. I can see mum is getting a little agitated as she keeps shifting in her seat.

'Well, it's gone from bad to worse. We haven't properly spoken to her for three months now which is not normal. We have spoken to Luke and he says she's happy but has become very dominating. She won't let him do his own thing, tells him how to dress and has told him he needs to go to the gym because he's not *toned* enough. And she's very controlling about time management. Always saying things like *get a move on, time is of the essence and time's ticking.* She used to always be the one late for everything, not a care in the world about time, even late for her own wedding. Now she's got a schedule for everything!'

There it is again, *time's ticking.* She is obviously a control freak, but I know a different, more threatening meaning behind her time-ticking phrase. A shiver goes through my body which I try to hide. It's not the time or place to tell my parents about my uncomfortable encounters with Zoe or the threatening actions she's made towards me. My dad's on a roll so I let him continue to talk.

'She's also lost loads of weight apparently,' he continues. 'She's become self-obsessed and turned vegetarian! It's not right. She's also gone and spent all their savings on laser eye surgery! Without even consulting Luke!'

This sounds about right. Zoe won't be content until she's moulded my life into her ideal. I don't think she will ever be fully content. She was bored with Tom and now she has a new project. Poor Luke, he is perfect just how he is, he shouldn't have to change for her. I can't imagine him going to the gym. He's always been very active and fit, but he's not the muscular type by any means. And to spend all our hard-earned savings on herself is insulting.

When I last saw Zoe, I could tell she was losing weight. By the sounds of things, she's lost even more. She's succeeded where I failed many a time. She wasn't happy with my body, so she's changing that too to fit into her ideal.

Mum pipes up. 'What you told us back along, you know … about … switching …'

Her voice cracks. Please tell me I'm not dreaming, and this is actually happening. Are my parents finally realising what's happened?

Dad stokes his beard and says, 'what your mum is trying to say is, we believe you.'

23

Family is a funny old thing. You don't always know what you've got until it's gone. Your family are the people who know you best, inside and outside. Parents raise children and it's the upbringing that moulds the child's future. Children dote on their parents, using them as guides into their new-found world. If an unexpected or inexplicable event occurs, family either pulls together or falls apart. I thought mine was falling apart, but now it seems it's gradually pulling back together again.

When my dad told me they both believed my story, I had an overwhelming feeling of relief. I broke down at their house, sobbing and telling them how much I loved them. I told them how relieved I was to know they believed my totally *un*believable story and that now they are back in my life, I feel the strongest I have done since the accident.

With my parents back in my life, Tom's ever-increasing presence and a new sister, I feel completely on the road to recovery. If I never go back to being Aisha, I know my life ahead will be happy.

Over the last month I have been thinking about trying to tell Tom again about what happened to me. So much time has passed that I don't know whether he will think me insane or if some kind of a realisation will dawn on him. It's clear to anyone who knew Zoe that I'm completely different, even though I look identical.

If I tell him, the positive outcomes would be that he believes me and loves me for who I am now. He could also get to know my parents and understand more about me and my life. But the negatives outweigh the positives. If I tell him, he may not believe me and send me for more treatment. Or he may believe me and leave me in pursuit of Zoe. Neither of which I want even a slight possibility of happening.

My marriage to Luke was comfortable. It was routine and I loved him dearly. But over the last month or so, I've regained that feeling of butterflies when someone walks into the room. Tom has such a presence. Yes, he is undeniably handsome, but it's his personality that really shines through.

Looks-wise Tom is not my type, at all. I've never gone for the macho, pretty-boy look. But I've learnt there's so much more to him. He's kind, compassionate, funny and ultimately loyal.

*

It's almost Christmas and I'm out shopping on a crisp December Saturday afternoon after finishing at *Young Stars* for the day. Mel has joined me to buy our last-minute presents. There aren't many people to buy for this year, but I need to get gifts for Tom, Mel, my parents and Tom's family whom I've yet to meet.

Mel still doesn't know the full story and as far as I'm concerned, she won't unless she has to. We get on so well now. We're so similar in so many ways; it's like meeting a soul mate.

'I'm off to go and get some Christmas cards in here,' I say to Mel.

Mel wants to go into the shop opposite, so I explain I'll either meet her in there when I'm finished, or she can come find me in the card shop if she finishes before me.

I'm searching through the *Mum and Dad* cards for a cute card, not one with flowers on or gardening tools. I always try to find the cutest one available and something that's personal to them. Then I get a tap on my shoulder.

'Blimey, that was quick!' I say as I turn around expecting to see Mel.

But it's not Mel. It's Gemma.

My best friend in the whole wide world is stood inches away from me, yet there is a vacancy in her expression.

'I didn't know whether to come over or not,' she says. 'I wasn't sure if it was you or not when I saw the bump, but I can tell I'm right by the way you're looking at me. I must be honest I did contemplate ignoring you.'

Part of me wishes she had. I haven't seen Gemma or spoken to her since she was supposed to meet me for a coffee, but Zoe turned up instead. She's my best friend, but I've healed so much since I last saw her, that I don't want her to un-do all the hard work I put in re-building my life.

'Why *are* you talking to me, Gemma?' I ask.

'I don't know really. Well yes, I do, what you told me ages ago, you know … I don't see Aisha anymore. We don't seem to get on. We just snipe at each other when we do meet up. It's not the same at all.'

Zoe really is making an impression on all the people in her life.

Seeing Gemma, it dawns on me. I never thought I could live without my best friend, but now I know I can. She didn't believe me when I needed her the most. She's different from my parents, my parents raised me, knew me inside and out, it means the world to have them back in my life. However, I now realise I don't need Gemma. She was someone I thought I could trust, someone who would believe anything I told her, and when I needed her the most, she abandoned me.

'I'm sorry, but I don't know what you think this has to do with me,' I say. 'I told you what happened to me, but you didn't believe me. If you'll excuse me, I have shopping to do with my sister.'

Wow, I feel so unbelievably strong. It felt great to say that!

'Look, I need you,' Gemma says. 'I need my best friend back, and I believe you now. I'm pregnant too!'

My best friend is pregnant. We always talked about when we'd have children and we hoped we'd be pregnant at the same time as each other. We shared all the big events in life and hoped this would be another. But now it's happening, I don't want a part in it. There's a big part of me that doesn't care anymore.

'I'm sorry, I can't do this.' I say. 'You abandoned me when I needed you the most. I thought you of all people would see me for who I am. I'm happy for you, I really am, but I can't be a support for you. Too much has happened. Too much has changed. I wish you all the best Gemma, I really do, but I must be on my way.'

She looks so hurt and lost but I meant every word I said. I've moved on and don't feel I need her anymore. She now needs me, but I can't give her what she needs. For once in my life, I'm going to be selfish and concentrate on me and my babies.

'Aisha ... *Aisha*!' She cries as I walk away.

I turn around and holler back, 'You can't pick and choose when you need me Gemma. As best friends, we were supposed to be there for each other, no matter what. I no longer trust you for not being there when I needed you the most … so we're done.'

With that I scarper into the shop opposite to find Mel, out of Gemma's sight.

Seeing her again didn't leave me longing for my past or feeling sad. If anything, I felt nothing. That was the sure sign that I am healing. If she believes my story, then it's up to her to rebuild our friendship. It's sad to leave the past behind, but that's exactly what I need to do.

*

When I get home, Tom has been decorating the house. He's bought a Christmas tree for the lounge, covered it with every coloured bauble under the sun and laced the branches with gold and silver tinsel. All the walls are covered with Christmas cards and bunting. It's our own magnificent grotto.

It's nice to have Tom home when I walk in. Recently he's been out and about more, as I don't need him so much. It's been good to see him living his life and not living it for me. But I have felt a little concerned.

There have been little things happening recently. He's had phone calls which he leaves the room to take or says he's busy and he'll phone them back, conveniently when I'm not around. He said he was going to the gym the other day and when I called him at the gym to say I was going to be late home and would bring a take-away with me, they told me he hadn't been in work all day. Whenever I ask him about it, he makes up some excuse or other.

Tom doesn't strike me as the kind of bloke who would have an affair. He's been through it himself and I don't think he would put someone else through the same suffering. Plus, we've been getting on so well of late I couldn't imagine him needing or wanting an affair.

However, there is one thing I haven't been giving him, sex. I don't feel it's the right time yet to move our relationship onto that level. When the time's right, I'll let him know. But maybe he's getting tired of waiting and bored of our platonic relationship. Perhaps he's felt the need to stray.

There's a pile of unopened cards on the coffee table which he's been waiting to open with me.

I make us both a coffee and settle down next to him in our winter wonderland, ready to open the remaining cards.

There were five in total before I made the coffee. I'm sure of it. But now there are only four.

'Have you opened one already?' I ask.

Tom leans forward on the sofa his body language going on the defensive. 'No, I've been waiting for you.'

I could have sworn there was an extra card. But I let it pass and enjoy opening the remaining ones with Tom. There are three from people at the gym, people I don't know. The other is from his parents.

'You don't talk about your mum and dad much,' I say. 'I know I wasn't ready to see them shortly after the accident, but it would be lovely to see them again soon. It may be a bit awkward as I don't remember them, but I'm sure they'll understand.'

Tom isn't overly close with his family. He doesn't see them very often, may be once or twice a year. There have never been any big fallings-out, it's just how his family works.

'We'll meet up at some point,' he replies.

That's all he ever says.

'Are they angry with me for what I did to you?' The thought suddenly dawns on me.

Tom clasps his hands over mine and says, 'They know what happened. I'll be honest, they thought I was stupid for taking you back. But they know you're expecting and are happy for us. Perhaps we'll meet up soon. They did seem genuinely worried after your accident.'

I would like to meet them. I feel I've gotten to know Tom so much in recent months, that to meet his family will cement our relationship further.

Tom has been acting shiftily since I entered the room. I thought it would be nice to open the cards together and bond. But he looks vacant, as if he wants to be somewhere else.

'I need to ask you something.' The time has come to ask him outright. 'I know we haven't been *close* since the accident, and I know men have needs. I know I'm not fulfilling yours if you get what I mean and …'

'What are you asking?' Tom looks hurt. Oh God, I've overstepped the mark. It's all in my head, it must be. But I have to know for definite even if I do come across as a paranoid idiot.

'Is there anyone else? I mean I wouldn't blame you as such, I've done it to you, and you've been so patient with me, I can't help but think maybe your patience is running out.'

'Oh my God! No!' He turns around on the sofa to face me and clasps my face in his hands. 'I would *never* do that to you, ever. I love you too much for that. You know I will wait for you. Please, please don't think that anymore.'

His mobile rings where he left it in the hallway, its timing impeccable. I give Tom a nod and he gets up to answer it.

He seemed genuinely surprised at my accusation. He couldn't possibly act that well. From what I know of Tom, he would never have an affair. Although, I must admit to myself that I don't know him that well. Perhaps he is planning a surprise for me.

Whilst he's on the phone, I look around at all Tom's handiwork. He's really done a fantastic job on the lounge. There's a log fire burning making it a lot cosier. The glow of the fire bounces off the tinsel on the tree, making it sparkle. This is the work of a man who cares, a man who wants to make his wife happy. This isn't an act of a man with something to hide, is it?

The messy torn-open envelopes on the coffee table ruin the effect of the room so I take them to the bin. As I discard them, I notice a Christmas scene torn in two in the bin. It's the other Christmas card. I knew there was another one, so why did Tom lie to me?

I pick it out of the bin and piece it back together, reading the message inside scrawled in my handwriting.

Happy Christmas to my darling husband. Thank you for meeting with me and listening to me. I hope that the New Year will bring us back together again, where we belong. Love as always, Z xxx

24

The bitch! She's upset everyone I've ever been close to and she's grown bored of my old life. So, she wants her old life back, now that I've finally accepted it as my future. What is she playing at?

And more to the point, what's Tom playing at meeting up with her and not telling me. Does he know what happened? Does he believe she is Zoe? If he does, then that will mean he knows I'm not his wife.

Although I feel I can trust Tom, I still don't know him as well as I did Luke. Luke was the only one I could trust with my life, but I lost him to her. Now she's cast him aside once she got bored of her new toy.

My heart suddenly goes out to Luke. He thinks he has a loving wife at home, someone he trusts implicitly, but he doesn't. His life has changed completely since the accident, it must have because of her and how she now treats him. Perhaps she'll leave him. Perhaps things will go back to how they were. I may never get my body back, but maybe I'm destined to return to Luke and Zoe's destined to return to Tom.

But would I want this? I honestly don't know what I want. For so long now, my old life has been completely out of my reach. It lay firmly in the past. But for the first time since the accident, I'm starting to think perhaps it can lie in the future again.

I was starting to think that Tom and the twins were my future. But, if he believes Zoe, he'll take her back, I'm sure of it. Zoe will leave Luke, which would give me the opportunity to persuade him to believe my story. After all, my parents believe me, and Gemma has shown signs of coming around to the idea. It's a possibility that Luke could too. I know I won't look like the person he fell in love with, but he may grow to accept my new image.

But what about the two mites growing inside me, will Tom and Zoe want to take them from me? Of course, they will, the twins aren't mine, I will have no rights over them.

However, DNA will show I am their mother, after all my body conceived them, so I would have something to fight with. But would Luke want to play stepdad? I just don't know.

How am I supposed to act when he comes back into the room? Should I question him, ask him what he knows, or do I need to know more before I act. I've never been a confrontational person. I normally dwell on things, bottling them up, until I need to say something, before I burst.

The lounge door opens, and Tom re-joins me on the sofa. He seems even more agitated throwing his mobile onto the coffee table. Was that her calling?

I decide to try to act as normally as I can, but I will get to the bottom of this. It's not just me that I need to protect but the two little ones inside me too.

*

This is my chance. Tom's gone for a bath and his mobile is still on the coffee table where he left it. It goes against everything I stand for, but I must know. I grab the mobile, settle down on the sofa and firstly check his recent calls.

The last call he received was from someone saved under the name 'Z' and I can see several calls made to the same number dating back two weeks.

I start to trawl through his text messages inbox. There are nine messages from Z in total.

They show *her* trying to contact him, explaining who she is, asking to meet him and arranging to meet with him at *their* favourite bar in town.

Then four days ago, the messages show her thanking Tom for meeting with her, pleading with him to believe her, declaring her love and reminiscing about their past, their wedding and their bedroom antics.

There seem to be no messages from Tom to her. But there are phone calls made by Tom to her, so I don't know what his responses were. I can only imagine the worst.

Rage circles through my head and down to my hands, I throw the mobile across the room whilst letting out a pained gurgling scream. I break down into full hearty sobs.

After letting out my final sob, I wipe away my tears and try to bring myself together. I can't let Tom know I know. I must keep the pretence for the time being. If he's going to kick me out and bring *her* back here, I need to make sure I have somewhere to go. I need to make sure I'm OK and my babies are OK.

I pick the pieces of mobile phone up from the far wall and put them back together again. Oh, please work, I can't have broken it. I press the 'on' button, and thank goodness, the screen lights up again. Carefully, I place it back on the coffee table where I left it.

Outside the bathroom door, I clear my throat and try to control my voice as I say, 'I'm just popping out, Mel's just texted. She wants me to pop round. I won't be long.'

With that, I grab my handbag and leave. I need to think things over.

*

The latch on the big wooden door clatters and the cast iron hinges creak as I open it. The winter evening sun shines through the stained-glass windows casting multi-coloured rays across the altar.

I've been to this church more in recent months than I have over the last few years. It has a calming effect on me allowing me to mull over recent events.

Every time I come here now, the memories of my wedding to Luke flood back. That was the happiest I'd ever been, I never thought I could be so happy again, such fond memories that will never leave me.

After my accident, all I wanted was to feel that happiness again, with Luke. The comfort and safety of our relationship was what I needed the most. I tried to tell him, tried to explain what happened, but he shut the door in my face. He believed *her* instead of me. I mean, why wouldn't he? I was now a stranger to him.

But there's a big part of me that thinks he may believe me now. The way Zoe treated him since the accident can't have been good. Both my parents and Gemma have told me their relationship is in tatters. No wonder, as she's not interested in making it work with Luke anymore, she wants Tom back.

The journey through life is never quite what you imagine it to be. It doesn't matter how much you plan and map your life out ahead of you, sometimes things happen which you have no control over. Things happen for a reason, but often you never saw that reason coming.

Even though I believe I now stand a chance of convincing Luke, I'm not sure that's what I want anymore. I never thought for one second I would ever fall in love with another man. It wasn't a thought that would have ever entered my mind, until now.

The old cliché, you don't know what you've got until it's gone, rings through my head, in more ways than one. I didn't know what I had with Luke until it was gone, not really. Of course, I loved him, and he knew I did, just as I knew he loved me. But I don't think you truly appreciate the good things in life until they're taken away.

The same now applies to my relationship with Tom. I haven't fully allowed Tom into my world. Likewise, I haven't fully allowed myself into his. But there are feelings I haven't felt for a long time that have re-surfaced during my time with Tom. He makes me feel special, valued and loved in a way I haven't for years. Perhaps in a way I've never felt before.

Knowing that all this could end shortly is heart-breaking. I love Luke and love the memories I have. But I know now that I have fallen in love with Tom.

They are both totally different, literally opposite ends of the male spectrum. Both of them are beautiful inside and outside but in completely different ways. Both of them love me but one loves me for who I am and the other loves me for what I appear to be.

Even though Tom loves me for what I appear to be, if it ever came to the point where I had to choose between the two of them, I know undoubtedly, I would choose Tom.

*

As I open the front door, I hear voices. They seem to be coming from the lounge. When I left Tom, he was in the bath, in the house alone. But now it's clear someone's here with him. I can hear a female voice.

Zoe. What the hell is she doing back here?

I try to walk as quietly as possible towards the lounge, straining my ears to catch what they're saying.

Tom's voice is too low a mumble to hear properly, whereas Zoe's is clear as day, high pitched and familiar.

'I love you, you believe me, don't you?' She says. 'Please. Just give me a chance. I've changed since the accident. I never appreciated you, not as much as I should have. You know me, inside out, come on and give me another chance.'

Tom mumbles something but I can't make out what he's saying.

Whatever it was, it pushed one of Zoe's buttons and she snaps. 'Just kick her out! She doesn't belong here anyway. It's not her house. She can just piss off back to her drip of a husband. I don't give a shit about her I just want to be back here with you.'

At which point I barge into the lounge. I look at Tom then I look at her, and then back at Tom again.

I am so angry. All the hurt, the anger of the past five months has accumulated into one big fireball of rage in my gut.

'What the hell's going on?' I shout. 'What do you think you're doing coming here, shouting the odds, marking your territory? You lost your right to do that when you abandoned your husband to shack up with mine!'

Zoe shouts back, 'You're welcome to that wimp of a man, go back to him, back to where you belong. I want my house back, all my lovely things back, my money back and my husband back. Go on, go, time's ticking Aisha!'

'Enough of this *time's ticking* Zoe!' I shout back at her. 'You don't need to threaten me, I'll go. I'll leave you to your happy lives together.'

Under my breath but clearly enough for Tom to hear, I mumble, 'How could you see her behind my back Tom? And to think I was starting to trust you … to fall for you.'

I run upstairs as quickly as my pregnant body will take me, tear open the door to the walk-in wardrobe, grab my suitcase and start flinging all my clothes into it. That's it, it's over. Whatever I had with Tom it's finished. Tears roll down my cheeks.

I can hear someone charging up the stairs and across the hallway to the bedroom after me.

'What are you doing?' Tom shouts. 'Please, don't go. Stay here … at least until you've sorted out somewhere to go.'

Somewhere to go, is he serious? He's really going to take her back after everything she's done to him. There's no way I'm going to stay here, I know my parents will take me in, they'll look after me.

I say nothing back to him. I just grab my bag, with tears in my eyes and flee back down the stairs.

She's waiting at the bottom of the stairway for me and blocks my exit leaving me trapped and balancing on the bottom step.

Zoe laughs directly and purposely in my face. 'You really think you could have my life? I feel so sorry for you. Your life was so pathetic that you had to steal mine?'

'I wanted it back, you know that! But you wouldn't let me. But now you're bored living my life, you come crawling back to Tom, well more fool him!' I shout back at her.

'Bored? Bored? Oh, you really have no idea, do you?' She sneers.

What the hell does she mean?

Tom runs down the stairs behind me and stands between us.

'Leave it Zoe,' he says. 'Look at her, she's pregnant and doesn't need this added stress.'

'Are you actually sticking up for her?' She replies. 'She's been fooling you since the accident, pretending to be me. She's carrying *our* children! I've a right mind to stab her in the stomach, get rid of the little *shits*. I never wanted them. Well, I was going to get rid before the accident, perhaps I need to keep trying!'

'That's enough Zoe!' Tom shouts.

'But you said yourself, you believe me! Are you choosing her over me? Seriously? Are you going to throw away years of marriage to be with her?'

Tom's silence only adds to Zoe's rage.

She continues, 'Well, if that's really the case, that you'd prefer to shack up with that pregnant bitch, then do it. But I tell you now, if you choose her then you lose my money. That's right, it's *her* or the money.'

My head starts swirling and I grab onto the banister for support. My legs start to tremble beneath me.

'Oh, that's right!' Zoe shouts looking directly at me. 'Playing the vulnerable-pregnant- woman card, are we? You think the only reason why I'm back here is because I'm bored and sick of being skint? Well, there's more. Your darling husband, the one you think you love and that *loves* you back, has been cheating on you for two years and you haven't got a clue!'

What? Luke? No, he wouldn't do that. Of course, he wouldn't, she's purposely trying to wind me up, trying to hurt me.

My knees start to wobble, my grip of the bannister is failing but through sheer determination my voice remains strong. 'What are you talking about, Zoe?' I ask. 'Just because you're a cheat it doesn't mean everyone is. Besides, who is he supposed to be cheating on me with?'

Zoe smiles, a wicked twisted know-it-all smile and says, 'Your best friend.'

Part 4

25

My grip fails and I lose my balance. A pain rages through my lower abdomen and I fall off the bottom step onto my hand and knees.

Tom grabs my sides and tries to help me back to my feet. 'Are you OK?' He asks me.

Luke and Gemma? My darling husband, who I loved and was trying for a baby with and my best friend, the person I grew up with who used to mean everything to me. Could they really have been having an affair for two years? How would they have gotten away with it? I couldn't possibly have been that blind to have not seen it happening.

No, Zoe's just sticking the knife in. But then, why would she say that if she wants Tom back? She wouldn't make it up, because she would want me to go back to Luke so she could have Tom. I wouldn't go back to him knowing he was cheating on me. Zoe wouldn't say anything unless it benefitted her and increased her chances of getting back with Tom or if it hurt me.

Oh shit! Gemma's pregnant. No, it couldn't be his could it? No, life couldn't be that cruel surely. To make me pregnant in someone else's body and then my husband impregnates my best friend when we'd been trying to conceive together for so long without success.

I can't keep my eyes open. My consciousness is slipping away.

'Stay with me,' I hear Tom's kind voice saying. 'Zoe, call for an ambulance! Now!'

With that I collapse fully to the ground and lose all consciousness.

*

After waking up in a hospital again I undergo several routine tests and check-ups. The doctor seemed concerned to start with, keeping me in overnight but after ultrasounds and other tests, I'm given the all clear with strict orders to rest and relax.

How ironic. If only they knew what had been going on throughout this pregnancy, they would laugh as they told me to rest and relax. How on earth am I supposed to relax?

Of course, the doctors wanted to know if I'd been under any pressure recently or any avoidable stress. But I couldn't tell them what had happened. I wouldn't have known where to even start. Therefore, I just explained I'd probably been over doing things with *Young Stars* and other things.

Tom didn't leave my side the whole time I was at hospital. We didn't talk about the recent events. In fact, we didn't really talk at all, only about medical things to the doctor. Not a word to each other. But he was there which was encouraging. He was probably more there for the babies than me, but I was grateful for his company, nonetheless.

There had been no sign of Zoe since I woke up at hospital, thankfully. She must have skulked back to the rock she crawled out from. However, I know that this isn't the end of it. I know she will be back. She'll try anything to get her life back with Tom. If I've learnt anything about Zoe over the past few months, it would be that she likes to get her own way. She's spoilt and knows what she wants and how to get it.

The doctor had a quiet word with Tom, I assume to tell him to look after me and make sure I rest. He's none the wiser. All he sees is a husband and wife who's expecting. He doesn't see what goes on in our lives.

Tom rode in the ambulance with me to the hospital, so he calls a taxi company to come and fetch us. We're silent the whole journey home. The taxi driver probably thought we were a right pair. He kept trying to make conversation, but it resulted in yes and no answers from Tom, I remained silent and just stared out of the window. Every now and then I caught the driver's facial expressions in the rear-view mirror. I saw him rolling his eyes and snarling to himself. It just goes to show, you never know what people are going through and without knowing the facts you shouldn't really judge.

As we walk back into the house, everything is as it was. My packed bag is lying on its side at the bottom of the stairs with its contents leaking onto the floor. I don't know what I'm supposed to do, so I start picking up my clothes and piling them back into the bag.

'What are you doing?' It's the first thing Tom's said to me since being in the hospital.

To be honest, I don't know what I'm doing, but I assume nothing's changed, I still need to leave.

'What does it look like I'm doing?' I ask, taking the bag in my hand. 'Nothing's changed has it? I don't belong here Tom. You know that, as well as I do. I've never belonged here. Only I've known it for longer that's all.'

Tom gently puts his hand on mine, and slowly removes the bag from my grasp.

'I don't want you to go anywhere. You do belong here.'

'But I don't, not really. It's a façade Tom. It's not real. I really wanted it to be and honestly started believing this could be my future, *our* future, but the events of last night made me realise it can't be. Besides if I stay, you heard what she said, she'll bleed you dry and take all the money.'

Tom guides me into the living room and sits me down next to him on the sofa.

'Zoe … um … Aisha, look all I know is that I'm happy here with *you*. What happened last night made me realise what it is that I want. And that's you. I don't want her in my life anymore. The last couple of months I've been the happiest in a long while, and that's because of you. I'm sorry I met up with her behind your back. I just needed to find out for definite what happened. And as for the money, she can have it. We'll be OK, more than OK. I never liked having the money anyway as I always felt owned by her in some way. Look, I feel I need to give you an explanation about everything.'

I let him continue. I don't want to hear about his meetings with her, but I need to.

'When she first contacted me, I didn't want to believe it. But you were so different since the accident, and I remembered how you were shortly after. How you didn't remember me and how you thought you lived a different life. The doctors convinced me it was amnesia and a result of your coma, so I thought nothing more of it, until she contacted me out of the blue.'

'She knew things no-one else possibly could, things about me and about our relationship. Things you didn't know yourself, which previously I put down to amnesia. I truly am sorry for meeting with her behind your back, but I purposely didn't tell you anything as I didn't want you to worry. I needed to find out answers myself and then work things through in my own head. I hope that you forgive me.'

'How long have you known?' I ask. I know they'd been messaging and meeting for two weeks, but I wanted to hear it from Tom himself.

'About two or three weeks,' he replies. 'I'll be honest with you. At first, I thought I wanted her back. It was nice to reminisce but as time went on there was something in my mind that was screaming *don't go back, she's trouble, she's not worth it*. I've been so happy with you. She never made me as happy as you have. This is what I was trying to tell her last night when you came home. I was trying to tell her it was over.'

So that's what made her so angry. She thought she could worm her way back into Tom's life and win him over again. He took her back once before, after her affair, so she assumed he would take her back again. But when he told her he didn't want her back, she flipped.

Tom continues. 'When she was saying those spiteful things to you it just reinforced my feelings towards her and towards you. And then when you collapsed ...'

He shakes away the tears forming in his eyes. 'I was so worried about you and the twins. All I could think was I couldn't lose you, not when I'd just found you.'

There's a big feeling of guilt gathering at the pit of my stomach. Tom is apologising to me, but I'm the one who fooled him into thinking I was Zoe. It wasn't just the doctors; it was me too. I couldn't tell him for fear of rejection, but it doesn't stop me from feeling guilty.

'I'm sorry too,' I say. 'I wanted to tell you so many times. I tried at the start, but I just sounded mad. Then as time went on, my feelings towards you increased, and I just couldn't find a way of telling you. I was worried that either you'd think I was mad again and send me back to rehab, or you'd go back to Zoe and leave me. I was terrified of losing you myself.'

'I completely understand,' he says. 'I just can't begin to imagine what you've been dealing with since the accident. You lost absolutely everything and had no support. Does anyone else know?'

'They do now,' I say. 'The hardest thing was being rejected by my family. Remember when I stayed at that B&B for a while? Well, I spent a lot of my time trying to persuade my loved ones to believe my story. I tried to tell Luke (my husband) and my best friend Gemma, but they slammed their door in my face. I also tried talking to my parents, but they didn't believe me. But after a while, my parents came around to the idea, after seeing their daughter acting so weirdly, they finally believed my story.'

I continued to tell Tom everything else. I told him about bumping into Luke and Zoe at the supermarket, about researching the accident, meeting Zoe at the bar instead of Gemma. I told him everything and it feels great that everything is now out in the open and someone is finally listening to my story.

'Does Mel know?' Tom asks.

'No, I haven't told her. Again, there have been times I've longed to, but I just couldn't summon the courage to.'

'Well, we'll both tell her together at some point,' Tom says. 'I want you to know I'm here, and I'm not going anywhere. I love you, you're not on your own anymore.'

This can't be happening. Finally, someone is listening. The most enormous weight is lifted from me. As I look at Tom my stomach churns and my heart pounds. This man is everything I want and everything that I need. He's dealing with this brilliantly and is saying all the right things.

'Thank you,' I say. 'You don't know how much this means to me. But there's just one thing playing on my mind. How do I know for definite you won't go back to her? I mean, you share a history with Zoe, you've created twins with her. I can't risk getting hurt again. Finding out last night that my *husband* had been having an affair with my *best friend* for two years hurt but if you were to take me in and then choose her over me at a later date, that would hurt so much more.'

Tom turns on the sofa to face me and brushes my hair behind my ear, tenderly stroking my cheek at the same time.

'I can't promise I'll never hurt you,' he says. 'But I can promise I won't take Zoe back. I love you.'

I feel myself weakening to him. All I want to do right now is kiss him. Kiss him like my life depended on it, but I just can't let go.

'What if we change bodies again?' I ask. 'It happened once, what if it happens again? Will you love me then?'

Tom doesn't seem to be phased by my question. He just slowly shakes his head and a warm smile creeps over his face. 'When will you realise? How many times do I have to tell you? I love *you*, not her or how you look but *you.*'

With that he grasps my face in his hands and pulls me towards him. He plants a kiss on my lips, pulls away and looks deeply into my eyes as if asking if that was OK for him to do. I answer by kissing him back deeply and longingly.

26

Tom and I spent the whole night together in each other's arms. Finally, I felt like a loving wife again. Finding out Luke had been having an affair with Gemma surprisingly didn't affect me as much as I thought it would have. Perhaps this is because I have fallen in love with Tom.

Gemma is pregnant and possibly with Luke's child. Well good luck to them both. I feel so blessed and happy with Tom right now, that I'm actually happy for them. Even though Luke did the worst thing possible by cheating on me with my best friend, I really do believe it happened for a reason. Luke wouldn't have been happy with Zoe so perhaps in the great plan of the Universe, Luke was supposed to fall in love with Gemma, just like I was supposed to with Tom.

Sometimes in life you plan, and you plan for the future, but some things just aren't within your control. I'm certainly proof of that. The old cliché comes back to me, everything happens for a reason, however bad it seems at the time.

*

We haven't heard from Zoe for a few weeks which meant Tom and I could spend Christmas and New Year together. There's always the worry that she'll turn up on our doorstep or threaten me in some way, but so far there's been no contact.

It was hard telling Mel. One of the hardest things I've ever had to do, but Tom held my hand throughout. Mel and I had become so close, I felt awful when I had to tell her what I had been hiding.

At first, she didn't take it very well. She couldn't believe our story, but hearing it from the both of us, she put all the pieces of the last few months together and realised we were telling the truth. It took her a couple of days to really come around to the idea. She felt loyal to her sister which I understood, but eventually she was grateful to have found a best friend in me.

She was honest with me when she told me she'd met up with Zoe and heard her side of the story. It hurt at first as I didn't know what lies Zoe would have told her. But Mel saw for herself that Zoe hadn't changed and showed no remorse for her affair with Mel's husband. I felt sorry for Mel when she told me. She cried a bit. But told me Zoe had lost her chance to rebuild their relationship.

I've always loved Christmas. Even as an adult, I turn into the biggest kid on Christmas Eve. Tom found this really refreshing as Zoe hated Christmas. He told me that at the start of their relationship he tried so hard to make Christmas special for Zoe, but his efforts were always wasted. Over time he just gave up and Christmas just became another day.

This year was possibly the best Christmas yet. Tom and I were like children, so excited. He even came to Church on Christmas morning and met my parents. Mum and Dad were so understanding, considering Tom was a stranger to them, and it seemed they fell for his charms straight away.

We celebrated Christmas together as one big family. Mum, Dad and Mel came around for dinner. We opened presents in front of the fire in the afternoon and Dad fell asleep in front of the TV. We ate until our stomachs ached and Tom and Dad enjoyed a few whiskeys together. We played Pictionary as a family in the evening and laughed so much I thought I was going to go into early labour. It felt so normal, yet so fresh.

New Year was equally lovely. Tom and I spent it alone, eating crisps in front of the BBC fireworks display.

There was always the worry that Zoe would spoil it somehow, but thankfully we didn't see her or hear anything from her.

*

'What do you think of this one?' asks Tom.

He's pointing at a tandem-pram, reduced from one-thousand-five-hundred pounds to nine-hundred pounds in the January sale.

'Looks great to me, what a bargain!' I beam at him.

It's so exciting to be out and about with Tom, shopping for our little ones. Tom's arms are already straining under the weight of five shopping bags full of toys, clothes and baby necessities, but he's still so enthusiastic.

We've been in Cribbs Causeway for three hours and my back is killing me, but the day's been filled with giggles and excitement.

'Let's order it then,' he says. 'And then we'll make a move, you must be getting tired.'

I must admit, my bump is getting bigger and bigger, even doing the everyday menial tasks take their toll on my back and ankles. I am tired, but happy.

Tom's been decorating the nursery this last week. It's really starting to come together. All creams with pictures of teddy-bears circling the walls. We've been spoilt by Mum and Dad. They've bought us two pine cots with musical teddy-bear mobiles hanging over each one. Not long left before the twins arrive and there's still a lot to prepare.

We giggle like excited teenagers all the way home and lug all our buys up the stairs towards the nursery.

'What the …?' Tom gasps as he pushes the nursery door open. 'Don't come inside love. Stay where you are.'

What on Earth's the matter? If he thinks I'm going to hover outside when he's had that reaction, he's got another thing coming.

As I push the door open, the first thing I notice is a slat from one of the pine cots lying on the floor snapped in two. I continue to press into the room and see Tom sitting in the middle of the floor, shopping bags strewn around him, staring at the walls, each one in turn.

I follow his line of vision and gasp, clasping my hands over my mouth. The beautiful teddy-bear wallpaper has been ripped in several places, streams of it hanging from where it once lay. The two cots that Mum and Dad saved for have been desecrated, broken into shards, the mobiles softly humming their little nursery rhymes.

'There's only one person who could have done this,' Tom murmurs.

'But how? How would she have gotten in?' I ask. 'She doesn't have a key, does she? Does she?'

Tom slowly nods his head, colour draining from his face. 'She does.'

Bemused I ask, 'What do you mean? She wouldn't have a key, not for our home, it's impossible.'

'I'm so sorry,' Tom says looking at me with guilt written across his face. 'It's completely my fault.'

I feel a rage starting to bubble away in the pit of my stomach. Why would he give her a key to the house unless he wanted her to have one? Was he secretly planning for her to move back in? Had he been seeing her again behind my back?

Tom sees my face turn a shade of red. 'It's not what you think!' He says. 'She took the spare key the night you collapsed. I rushed off in the ambulance with you, it all happened so quickly I left without locking the doors or anything. She rang me to tell me and that she would use the spare key to lock the house for us and post it back to us. I'm so stupid! I just thought it was a kind thing for her to do and then I forgot she had it.'

He spreads his arms, taking the horrific scene into his grasp, 'This is down to me!'

'No, no it isn't,' I try to soothe him. 'It's totally that scheming bitch's fault. Look at it! Did you take a hammer to the cots? Did you rip the wallpaper off? No! It was her, not you. OK, yes it was a silly thing to do, but I understand why you did it.'

'I'm so sorry,' he says again. 'We need to phone the police. She can't do things like this. Enough is enough.'

We can't phone the police. If we do, the whole story will come out and they'll think we're insane or having a laugh, they won't believe it. Nothing will come of it. She'll walk away scot-free and be madder than ever.

'No,' I say. 'We can't. They won't believe us, and it will only make her even angrier. We can't get the key back, as she's probably already cut a copy. We just need to get our locks changed.'

I can see Tom is building up a rage of his own. I try to reassure him but he's adamant the police are the only way. I can't go through the added stress of an investigation or worse scenario a court case, not in my condition. Therefore, I plead with Tom not to go to the police. It's too much of a risk to the babies.

'Well, if we don't go to the cops, I'm going to her,' he says. 'This can't go on. I can't have you scared in your own home or stressed out. She has to be told, once and for all.'

Tom grabs his mobile, car keys and storms into the garage. I follow him, begging him not to go, but he ignores me. I haven't seen him this angry before. That woman has such a hold on our relationship. To think thirty-minutes ago, we were blissfully happy, preparing for our future together and now, yet again, we're distraught by her actions.

'Please, please don't go,' I cry. 'Let's just get the locks changed and go back to being happy. Please?'

'Do you really think we can do that Aish? While she's still holding all the cards, there's no chance. She has to be stopped.'

'Well, in that case, I'm coming with you.'

Before he has a chance to argue, I strap myself into the passenger seat. I can see him in the wing mirror, looking flustered. He walks around to the driver's seat, straps himself in and says, 'OK, but I'm doing the talking.'

*

Such familiar settings loom up ahead of me. This was my house with so many dreams of it becoming a family home. I feel sad but only because I feel sorry for the old me, the old me who was so unaware of how my dreams would unravel and what terrors awaited me. But I also pity my old self because I thought I was happy. I thought this house was my centre of everything. I thought Luke loved me and my life was perfect. I didn't have a clue.

I thought I was happy back then and I thought I was in love. I know now that it wasn't love, it was comfort. It was what I knew, and it was regime. I've never loved before how I love now. Every time I look into Tom's eyes my stomach flips and a warm feeling travels through my veins. He has a way of showing his love for me without doing or saying anything, he just has to look at me with those big brown eyes and I know.

Every inch of me wants to stop Tom from entering the house. I want to protect him from her and even himself. He's never been this angry before, at least not that I've seen. It just goes to show what she does to him.

Tom bangs on the door with such an angry force, I see the door shake in its frame.

'I know you're in there!' He shouts and bangs. 'Come on Zoe, come out!'

I try to calm him, telling him the neighbours will complain if he keeps this up, and she won't come out if she feels threatened. But my words fall on deaf ears.

'We're not going anywhere until you open this door!' He continues.

Faint sounds of shuffling come from the inside. 'Go away!' I hear her shout. 'You're not coming in.'

Tom goes to shout again but I elbow him sharply and whisper, 'No'.

'Zoe, please open the door,' I say as calmly as I can muster. 'Please. We just want our key back and then we'll leave you alone.'

Silence falls for a couple of seconds and then a key turns slowly in the lock and before the door can open fully, Tom wedges his foot inside and barges through the doorway. Zoe has no choice but to let us both through.

27

'How dare you just barge in here,' Zoe screams. 'Get out!'

'Not until this is finished! Once and for all,' Tom yells back.

Tom strides through the hallway straight into the kitchen.

Before either one of us can stop him, I can see Tom's rage heighten. The kitchen table gets up-turned, its contents crash across the floor and the chairs fly out around him. His kind gentle hands turn into ravaging tools sending all the plates and cutlery from the sink drainer, clattering and smashing onto the cold tiled floor. He grabs a set of china plates ready to launch them at Zoe's face.

I know Tom wouldn't hurt her, he wouldn't hurt anyone, this was just his passion and frustration, but I can't watch him do this to himself anymore.

'Stop!' I yell. 'Enough is enough! This isn't the Tom I know.'

I turn to face Zoe. 'Look! Look at what you're doing to him, what you've already done to him. This has to stop now!'

But Zoe's clearly not in the mood to let this drop. 'Go on then,' she screams in Tom's face. 'Do it! If you hate me so much go on, throw them at me!'

I can see Tom's hands shaking violently, the plates being gripped so tightly his knuckles turn white. Without giving it a second thought, I lunge between Tom and Zoe blocking his target.

'This is not right Tom,' I say. 'Put the plates down! Otherwise, it's not just Zoe who'll get hurt.'

His knuckles slowly regain their colour, and his grip loosens.

'That's it my love,' I say calmly. 'Put them down, this isn't you. You need to calm down.'

I move slowly towards him and gently take the stack of plates from his grasp and place them on the table. I pick up one of the over-turned chairs and usher Tom to his seat.

'I wouldn't have done it, I wouldn't have,' Tom stutters. 'I wouldn't want to hurt her … I just … just feel so angry.'

Zoe bursts into hysterical laughter.

I swing round and shout at her, 'What the bloody hell is so funny?'

She stops laughing but keeps the smile on her face looking directly at Tom. 'Don't you miss this love? This passion? You used to love it! This is what we're about. If we were still together, we'd probably be ripping each other's clothes off by now and racing up to the bedroom. Well, we still could! Run along now Aisha, Tom and I want to play.'

Tom starts to stand to launch another attack, but I forcefully place my hand on his chest and push him back down into the chair, wrapping my arms around him.

'Look at you,' Zoe continues. 'You're pathetic!'

'I wouldn't touch you again with a barge-pole,' Tom shouts.

Zoe stops. She looks herself up and down. 'Of course, you wouldn't! Look at me! I'm not exactly God's gift to mankind. No wonder you wouldn't, no man would, including Aisha's so-called husband!'

She continues. 'I've tried to sort this body out, lost a bit of weight, styled my hair. But it's useless. I can't make shit look good! The only way to get you back is if I get my body back, with or without the horrendous bump. That's the only reason you 'love' Aisha, because she looks like me!'

'She's twice the woman you'll ever be!' Tom snarls at her from beneath my grasp. 'She's the mother of my children, not you! She's kind, funny, loving. Everything I searched for from you but could never find.'

'You really think that? That's not what you were saying a few weeks back when you made love to me, right here in Aisha's bed!'

What? No, no he wouldn't have. My grasp loosens and my knees wobble. Tom springs from his chair to take hold of me, but I push him away and slump to the floor.

'She's lying. I swear to you,' he says. 'How could I? I love you.'

He turns to face Zoe. 'You will pay for this. You just can't help yourself from being bitter and twisted.' He moves towards her.

'It's a fantasy in your head!' He shouts, inches from her face. 'I don't want you. I haven't for a long time. I love Aisha get it through your head. Please!'

Zoe looks overcome. It seems the realisation finally dawns on her that it's over. 'Get out!' She screams. 'Get out, get out, *get out*!'

'Let's go,' He says in his normal, kind Tom voice. 'We need to get out of here before even the air poisons us. We'll just get new locks. She won't bother us again. I won't allow it.'

I know she's lying and trying to cause problems between us. Every inch of me trusts Tom, if anyone's the cheat, she is. Gratefully, I take Tom's arms as he helps me to my feet.

Zoe stands in the kitchen doorway, blocking the exit. 'You know what Aisha? I found out the other day that we both died and were resuscitated at exactly the same time that day. Our souls must have floated around that hospital for a moment, only to be sucked back into the wrong bodies. It can't be too difficult to re-enact that!'

Tom pushes past Zoe, ignoring her completely and just focuses on the front door guiding me behind him with his hand. As I pass Zoe, she whispers in my ear quietly enough to go unnoticed by Tom. But I hear it as clear as day.

'I will get my body back, even if it means killing you in the process,' she says.

As Tom pulls me through the door, I turn my head round to see Zoe standing there, composed and poised with her finger raised to her head. Her sinister *I'm watching you* point follows me as I'm taken to safety.

*

There are many negative emotions I've felt since the accident. I've felt sad, worried and helpless, lost and even threatened sometimes. But I have never felt fear, until now. Fear is the strongest one yet, fear of losing everything, fear of losing my babies, and fear of losing my life.

There have been times when I've been scared. Being alone in the world is a very scary ordeal. Losing those you love is a scary thing. But never fear. Right now, I'm terrified for my life and terrified for my babies' lives.

During the car ride back, I can feel a dull ache in my lower abdomen. It's almost as if the twins feel my fear and echo it in response.

Could what she said really be possible? My faith believes that our souls leave our bodies once we die. I know we both had to be resuscitated but really, what are the odds that we were resuscitated at exactly the same time?

If this really did happen, it can't have been down to chance. Call it what you may, whether it be God's plan, divine intervention or fate. Whatever the terminology, it happened for a reason.

I believe there are a few reasons why this happened. I never would have met my soulmate and I never would have been a mother to two children. I also believe it happened so the twins have a mother who loves them and will care for them throughout their lives.

If Zoe really thinks she can re-enact what happened in order to get her body back, I must be strong and stop her, whatever it takes. I must protect these babies.

Several months ago, when I wanted my old life back and before I knew the kind of person Zoe was, I would have been more than happy to work together with her in order to switch back. I don't know if we would have found a safe way to do it or not, but we could have done it together.

It was she who stopped me from trying to switch back. Her selfishness is what will cause her own demise. If she'd worked together with me from the start, perhaps we would have swapped back by now. But, like I said before and will keep saying, everything happens for a reason. I swapped with Zoe, rather than anyone else, so that I wouldn't get my old body and life back. This is where I belong.

So now to know everything is being threatened, makes me terrified. I cannot and will not allow her to do anything to ruin what I have now.

*

'I honestly didn't do what she accused me of,' Tom pleads once we've got home. 'I just couldn't do something like that.'

I know he's innocent, he must be. Besides, Zoe contradicted herself during her bitterness earlier. I spent the drive home thinking enough about everything that had just happened. In one breath she says Tom only loves me because I have her body, yet in the other she says he finds her so attractive that he sleeps with her. It doesn't make sense.

'I know,' I say but I'm not as happy as I should be. Tom became a different person earlier and I can't help thinking what he would have done to her if I hadn't been there. 'I believe you. You've believed everything I've told you in the past, and I believe you now. I know you wouldn't do that.'

Tom looks confused. I'm saying the right thing, but I just can't hide the fact that his earlier actions scared me.

'Thank you,' he says reaching out to hug me. I flinch. 'What? What's the matter?'

'What was that back there?' I ask him, feeling my heart start to pound. 'You really scared me. I didn't know what you were going to do next! What if I hadn't been there to stop you? You would have kept going and goodness knows what else you would have done.'

Tom backs away and lowers his head, a red flush travelling the surface of his cheeks. 'I'm sorry you had to see that. I was just so angry. She knows what buttons to press. She always has. Even though she's poison, I'd never hurt her. I lost it back then and it even scares me when she brings that side out of me.'

'I'm not surprised! That wasn't you Tom and I tried to tell you to stop, I tried to protect you …' my words fail me, and I start to sob.

'I was just so angry. I wanted to protect *you,* that's why I flipped like I did.'

He's stronger than he thinks, and I'm not used to a man being so protective of me. My heart warms again, knowing that he really does love me.

Tom reaches out to hug me again, and this time I let him.

He kisses my neck and moves his lips up my cheek and towards my lips. Pulling away he says softly, 'I love you. I'll never make you feel that way again, I promise.'

I look into his eyes and I know he's being honest with me. I know he would never do anything to hurt me or the twins. This is the man I love.

My heart rate slows, and my tears dry up. Tom is there, he's shown he will protect me. But then I remember Zoe's leaving comment and my heart rate quickens again, the terrifying feeling rising to the surface once more.

'Arrrrrrrrgh!' A searing pain sweeps across my lower abdomen. I buckle under the shear agony holding my bump with both hands, gasping for air. A cold wet feeling comes from between my legs. I look at Tom through blood shot eyes and see his face has gone pale.

'We need to get you to the hospital. Now!'

L. A. Evans

28

The pain soars through my body rippling up towards my chest. I move one of my hands down my inner thigh and feel a thick liquid flowing down my leg. Bringing my hand up again I turn it round so the palm is facing me, and it's covered in blood.

I look around me. I am sat on the floor in a pool of the red stuff.

My first thought is that I am having a miscarriage. The second is that I am giving birth prematurely. Both options terrify me.

'What's … happening …. to me?' I say through staggered breaths.

Tom's rustling through his coat pocket and I hear the jingling of his car keys. 'You're OK my love. We just need to get you to the hospital.'

He places one hand on my elbow and the other around my waist and helps me to my feet. The walk to the car feels like a mile. Every step I take causes another bout of pain to travel up my torso. I pant and groan alternatingly the whole way to the car.

'Why ... aren't we ... getting an ... ambulance?'

Tom doesn't answer which worries me.

'I don't ... want to get ... blood in the car,' I continue.

'Don't worry about the car,' Tom says. 'Aisha, darling, there's not enough time to wait for an ambulance.'

Not enough time? What does he mean? How bad am I? I can't lose the twins, I just can't. But I know something's wrong.

'It's ... too early!' I panic.

There's not one part of me that will let this happen. I've been through too much to get to this point, just for it all to have been for nothing. But what if I can't save them? Perhaps this is all part of the big plan. Maybe I was never supposed to have children, regardless of what body I'm in.

Tom helps me into the car but sitting down is too painful, so I try to get back out again. 'I can't! It … hurts!'

'You have to Aish, come on, you're going to be fine, but we have to get you there now.'

Tom talks to me constantly, reassuring me that I'm going to be OK and so are the twins, but I don't believe him. Not after seeing all that blood.

He closes the passenger door, trapping me inside. I must be strong. I can't give up, if I do, I'll be giving up on my two little mites who right now need me more than ever. I must find inner strength that I've never had to draw on before. I can't lose them, I just can't.

Engine started, the roof is still down, the cold air strikes my already trembling skin. Tom ramps up the heating but refuses to put the roof up saying there's not enough time. As we pull up at the bottom of the drive, I see a familiar car parked up the road. Inside, I see an even more familiar face. Zoe.

I try to point, try to get Tom's attention, but all I do is freeze in time. What's she doing here? It's as if she's been waiting for us.

We hurry out onto the road. In the wing mirror, I can see her pull out behind us, keeping her distance. Tom's foot is firmly on the pedal accelerating far too quickly, taking the corners too sharply.

The radio is still playing which I try to focus on to take my mind away from the pain, but there is too much static to make out any words. The radio station needs re-tuning, but I can't reach it.

I jerk forward as, what I can only imagine is a contraction, rears its ugly head and I let out a gargling cry grabbing my bump in a useless act of protection.

As it subsides, I start to pant, trying to control my breathing as I was taught in antenatal.

My eye catches another glimpse of my old car still closely following us. Her horn beeps once, twice, three times. The fourth time, she keeps her hand on the horn letting out a long, almighty baaaarp.

She's got Tom's attention. I can see him looking in the rear view and then wing mirror. A look of panic spreads across his face. His gaze flits between both mirrors and the road intermittently, back and forth, back and forth.

Zoe's accelerating now, her front bumper almost touching our back. I can see her face and her expression is wild but determined.

'She's … trying to … kill us,' I manage through gasps.

Tom looks in his rear-view mirror. 'Shitting hell!'

The car jerks as Tom changes to a lower gear in order to accelerate further.

I grab onto the dashboard with one hand and grip my seatbelt with the other, fixated on the wing mirror.

Zoe swerves in a zig-zag fashion, trying to overtake us, beeping the horn as she goes. Cars travel past us in the opposite direction, beeping their own horns and flashing their lights in their own panic.

We take a bend in the road sharply and the wheels screech on the tarmac causing the car to sway and skid, but Tom regains control and accelerates once again.

This causes Zoe to fall behind slightly, but I can see her intent is regained as she too accelerates back up towards our rear.

Another wave of contraction pain flows through me, they're getting closer together, if that's what they are. I've never felt pain like this before. It stabs with every breath.

The static on the radio starts to clear and music begins to play, loudly. It helps to shift my focus. It's playing the end of a song that seems familiar. It's the song from my dream.

I had much on my mind and no way to turn,
I'll never go back, must keep moving on.
The hurt that I feel deep inside of my soul,
Vanished from my new intrepid form.
I will not return

To my life before.

I will not return

To my life before.

In the distance I see *the* crossroads. I know this junction too well and try to shout to Tom to stop. Please, stop! My body shakes, gasping for air but the car rockets on. Another contraction takes hold and I cry again. My head whirls, I think I'm going to be sick.

Before I know it, a mouthful of vomit is splayed across the dashboard. My eyes are sore from watering with the pain of every breath and my heart is racing. I hope that Tom will read my mind and stop the car. But the junction is still fast approaching.

I wipe my mouth and catch another glimpse of the maniac behind us. She swerves onto the other side of the road and increases her speed. She's overtaking us.

'Look … out!' I manage, through short breaths and panic.

As her car draws parallel to ours, we both look to the right and see her arms flailing and her lips shouting words we can't understand. She winds down the passenger electric window and over the song playing, I think I make out these words:

'I told you I'd come for you!'

Oh my God! She really is intent on killing me. My fears have become reality. She's going to kill us both and our babies.

Tom winds down his window and shouts back, 'What the bloody hell are you doing? You're going to kill us all!'

Then both Tom and I stare in horror as a car approaches on the other side. Zoe speeds up, faster and faster. She swings back over to our side in front of us. Her brake lights go on growing brighter and brighter as she approaches the junction. Tom stop! I yell in my head; the words won't come out.

'Shit, shit … *shit*!' Toms shouts as he slams his foot on the brakes.

Our brakes squeal, clawing into the tarmac. The car sways uncontrollably but we can't stop in time.

We slam into the back of her car, forcing her out onto the adjoining road.

My eyes automatically close, shielding me. But I don't want to be shielded, I need to know what's happening. Last time I was in a car accident, I didn't know what happened. I can't forget again. I must remember. I open them.

I see the road ahead rolling, trees and grass swirling round and round. We keep moving. The car isn't stopping. Please make it stop! I close my eyes again as I can't focus anymore.

This is it, the end. I've tried to be strong. I've tried to look after my babies. But I can't do any more. In a split second I see my parents and Mel in the darkness of my eyelids and try to reach for them, but they're not there. The car finally comes to a stop. I'm upside down.

I strain my neck to look at Tom, but his eyes are closed, and blood is oozing from his forehead. Oh my God, please no, he can't die! I must do something.

The windscreen is shattered; smoke is billowing out of the bonnet and tarmac lies beneath my head. Through the smoky haze I can just make out my old car in a hedge opposite, its back wheel still spinning.

I reach out to Tom who's lying perfectly still but my seatbelt tugs at my chest.

'Tom?'

'Tom?'

There's no response. I unclasp my seatbelt, move as best as I can towards him but from the pit of my abdomen a torturous throbbing surges through my veins. My arch enemy, darkness, materializes and I am consumed by it.

29

My index finger on my right-hand twitches. It sends a shiver through my rigid body. I can't move anything else. Open your eyes, I tell myself, open them. I feel my eyelids shudder under the effort, but they fail to open.

My mind is hazy, but I remember. I remember the accident, Tom's deathly silence and my twins. A feeling of dread spreads through me, please let them all be safe and alive. I try to move my hand to my abdomen. I need to feel my bump, need to see if they're ok, but my hand won't budge.

The strain of trying to move my hand causes my finger to twitch again. I feel the presence of someone by my side leaning over me; their perfume washes over me, sweet and floral.

She backs off and her footsteps scuttle away from where I lie.

I can hear her talking to someone else in the distance.

'She's coming around,' I hear the woman say.

The perfumed scent intensifies, meaning she's close by again.

'That's it, you're coming around and you're going to be OK. Can you open your eyes for me?'

My eyes flicker as I try to peel back my lids. My dry lips part slightly as I attempt to speak.

'Tom,' I croak. 'My babies.'

'Don't try to speak, just open your eyes for me,' she continues. Gradually I start to see light and the form of a woman in blue starts to take shape. 'That's it, you're doing well.'

As she comes into focus, I can see she's quite young with strawberry-blonde hair scooped back into a bun, a few wispy threads hang down in front of her face.

'Welcome back,' she smiles. 'I'm your nurse. My name's Nurse Watson but you can call me Donna.'

'I remember you,' I say.

Her face crinkles as if trying to remember me. I guess she sees a lot of people during her shifts so I wouldn't blame her for not remembering me. 'You were here last time I was in hospital. I had a car crash then too.'

She rustles through my notes. 'Um ... no, my love, your records say you saw a Nurse Benson last time you were here, but don't worry, lots of people get us confused.'

Nurse Benson? I don't think that was her name. Besides, unless Donna has a twin working with her in the same hospital, she must be mistaken.

'It was definitely you,' I say. 'You were so kind when I was so confused. I never really thanked you properly for all your support.'

Donna looks at me awkwardly. 'No, my love, you have me confused with Nurse Benson. I'll pass on your thanks to her though. Right now, you have to rest. You've been through a massive ordeal, and not for the first time this year by all accounts. You must rest.'

No, she's wrong. I've never seen a Nurse Benson before.

With every inch of determination, I have, I move my hand to my stomach. There's no bump. I start to panic.

'Where are my babies?' I cry. 'Did they survive?'

Concern flushes Donna's face and she starts checking the monitors. She places the back of her soft warm hand on my forehead.

'No, you don't understand,' I say. 'I was carrying twins. Zoe overtook us, the car crashed, Tom was hurt, and I must have passed out. Please, where are they?'

'OK, love, you're not making sense. Please try to stay calm. I can't stress enough that you've been in a serious accident and have just woken up. You must rest. It'll take you a while to come around properly and then everything will make a little bit more sense. You'll be OK.'

I'll be OK? Everyone said that to me last time and in the end they were right. Everything did turn out OK, it was more than OK. It was brilliant.

My chest tightens, I gasp for air, but my windpipe fails. I gasp again, wheezing. Donna bustles around me and places a nebulizer over my mouth to pump a cocktail of medicine into my lungs.

'Take deep breaths as deep as you can,' Donna calmly says. 'Try not to panic.'

I suck in the air frantically whilst staring into Donna's kind eyes. She smiles at me reassuringly and gradually my breathing slows into a normal pattern again.

'There we go,' she says. 'That's it, breath slowly. It's just your asthma, you'll be fine.'

I grab the mask and remove it from my face. 'Donna,' I say. 'Did I die in the accident?'

She looks confused.

'Was I brought back, resuscitated? Please it's important.'

She can see my panicked expression and shakes her head. 'I don't think that's of great importance ...'

'It is! You don't understand, I need to know.'

'Yes,' she sighs. She takes my hand in hers and says softly, 'You had such a blow to the head. Your breathing was faint when the ambulance arrived. When they moved you from the car you stopped breathing. The paramedics had to bring you back. And they did, which is fantastic news. So, rest now. You're going to make a full recovery.'

'How long have I been here?' I need to know.

'Two days,' she says. 'We've been monitoring you whilst you've been sleeping. Now you need to rest.'

Donna turns her back to leave the room.

'Donna? One more thing before you go.'

She twists her head round, a frown on her face. Her patience is waning.

'I need a mirror, please.'

'But why ...'

'Just get me one,' I say. 'Please.'

She nods and leaves to find one.

The hospital room is now empty and I'm alone again with only my thoughts for company.

I feel my belly again, hoping for some sign of the twins, but there's nothing.

The hospital bed sheets are crisp and white. Straining my right arm, I pull back the sheets and unwrap my body. The nurse has put me in one of those ultra-sexy gowns that gape in unsightly places. I have no idea where my clothes are. There's no jewellery, no rings, nothing.

My chest is moving up and down rapidly. I peek inside my gown and there, on my left breast is the pink fleshy scar left by Mrs Bishop.

If it weren't for Donna confirming I had been in another accident earlier in the year, I would have started to think this past year had all been a dream. But it hasn't, it can't have been.

Of course, no-one's by my bedside, they don't know it's me. My loved ones will be by Zoe's bedside, comforting her and loving her. And I bet she will love every second of it. Will she come clean? Will she tell them her plan worked and she succeeded in switching back? She may decide not to, and live as me, again.

I must be strong. There is no way she'll do this to me and my family again. I won't let her. I must get out of this bed. I must find my family and tell them what happened. I must know everyone's safe. I need to warn them all. She's unhinged and right now they could be falling for any of her lies. They believed me once before, they have to believe me again.

The last time I saw Tom he was not in a good way. What if he didn't survive? Not only could I have lost him, but what if the twins survived and she ends up raising them herself? I need to protect them.

I slowly slide my elbows up behind me to try and move into a sitting position, but there's hardly any strength in them. I have no idea what injuries I've suffered. Donna said I'd had a blow to the head. But I could have suffered from broken ribs, bruising, anything. I probably shouldn't be moving, but I must get up, I have to find my family.

As I'm struggling to sit up, Donna reappears in the doorway carrying a mirror. She sees what I'm doing and rushes over. She tells me I shouldn't be sitting up and that I need to rest.

'I need to go, I need to find my family,' I say.

'You're in no fit state,' she replies. 'Seriously Aisha, your accident was serious. You must understand. You almost died. You have to rest.'

Of course, I almost died. I wouldn't be in this situation if I hadn't. But the point is I'm alive and I must find my family before it's too late, before they fall for Zoe's lies again, before she hurts them.

I fight to sit up again; I won't do as I'm told. I haven't got time to rest.

Donna shakes her head but realises my determination. She presses a button on the bed which moves the pillow end up into a sitting position. This helps me immensely.

'Thank you,' I say.

Donna frowns. 'Well, it's obvious you won't do as you're told, so at least this way it won't do you as much harm. But don't you dare think of moving from this bed. I'll be back to check on you in a bit. Whilst I'm gone, please behave.'

She checks the machines and fittings before exiting the room, leaving the mirror on the bedside table.

I reach over to get it, swallow hard, and let out a long exhale of air. Here goes nothing.

As I hold the mirror up to my face, my freckles are as clear as day.

The mirror drops to the floor.

Voices loom from the corridor outside my room, loud and menacing.

'Please calm down sir,' Donna's raised voice echoing.

A man's voice shouts, 'I need to see her, she's going to pay for what she's done.'

It's Tom! He's alive thank goodness. Shit, he thinks I'm Zoe. That means he thinks I caused the accident.

'Tom?' I cry.

The door swings open, arms flailing through the opening. A security guard blocks his path, but I can see Tom's face over the uniformed man's shoulder. It's full of rage and tears. He looks at me with disgust, hatred and loss.

'I loved you once,' he shouts. 'I thought you loved me once too. How could you do this? How ...'

With a lot of scuffling and shouting, the security guard pushes Tom back out into the corridor, the door slamming shut behind him. Tom's shouting is no longer understandable, and it just turns into a muffled noise.

The door creaks open.

'Are you OK?' Donna asks as she peers in from behind the door.

I nod, wiping away the tears from my cheeks.

She pushes the door open and walks into the room. Alongside her are two police officers, one male, one female.

'This is PC …' she looks at the badges they're holding up to her face. 'Stanford and PC Marks. They just want to have a chat with you.'

She turns to them and says, 'She's still very poorly, so don't be long. She needs to rest.'

The officers take a seat by my bedside. Donna smiles a warm, reassuring smile and leaves me alone with them.

30

The police officers stayed for about ten minutes, until Donna came back in to ask them to leave. She could hear from outside that I was becoming distressed.

They told me that Tom had made allegations towards me, that I'd deliberately caused the accident through dangerous driving. All of which was true, it just wasn't me who was driving the car.

Of course, I couldn't say this to the officers. How on Earth could I have explained that it wasn't me driving the car, but I was actually the passenger in Tom's car? And then we switched bodies at the scene of the accident after previously switching bodies earlier in the year. That would have sounded ludicrous. And that's just what it is, madness.

They also told me that I could be facing charges related to the accident, but they didn't disclose what. But they were quite clear that the allegations made were serious and I had to co-operate fully in their investigations. I've never done anything against the law in the past, apart from maybe the odd parking ticket. And now I'm faced with this.

Alone in my room again, I ponder over the police questions. They asked me what happened during the accident. I couldn't exactly lie, and I didn't want to protect Zoe. But at the same time, I wasn't expecting to be the one being questioned. I said the only thing I could think of to say, which was that I stopped too quickly at the junction and the car behind me couldn't stop in time, pushing me out into the road.

They also asked what my relationship was to Mr. Young. I had to lie this time. I couldn't say I was his wife, or his lover, that would have raised too many unnecessary questions. So, I just denied knowing them.

I never imagined I would ever be in the situation to be questioned by the police, let alone lie to them. But how could I tell the truth?

I told them that I had heard that the woman in the other car was pregnant and asked them if they knew if they had survived. They wouldn't answer me. They just went on to the next question.

All I care about now is that Tom finds out the truth and that the twins survived. I don't care that I'm alone, facing charges, battered and bruised. None of that matters. All that matters now, is that I find my family.

The way Tom looked at me is embedded in my memory. He looked completely lost. It wasn't just anger in his eyes, it was sadness, grief. It was the way people look when they've just lost someone close to them. The hatred and anger are the first emotions to come through, then when that's passed, the sadness is all that's left.

If Tom is grieving, the likelihood is that one, if not both, of the twins had died. When I think of the pain that surged through me in the accident, I wonder how two unborn children could have survived that ordeal.

Donna left me in the sitting position. This makes it much easier to ease myself on to the edge of the bed. I must find Tom; I need to know if the twins are OK.

With both feet on the ground, I rip the wires from my body and shakily stand. My body gives and I grab onto the bedside table for support, the room spinning around me. I need to take control of this. Blinking madly, I try to regain focus and gradually put one foot in front of the other, using the wall as support.

The door opens. Every time. Donna has such impeccably bad timing.

'What are you doing? Get back in your bed, you're in no fit state,' her face as stern as my mother's.

'Please,' I beg. 'I need to know they're all OK. I feel like a prisoner here. I'm alright, honest, I've managed this far. Please.'

'I'm sorry,' Donna says. 'I have to insist that you get back into bed. You are *not* well enough yet to be gallivanting around the hospital.'

She takes my elbow and slips her other arm around my waist, guiding me back to the bed. I try to fight against her, but my body is weaker than my mind.

'But I have to know,' I insist.

Donna eases me onto the bed and hooks up the wires again.

'Look, I'll try and find out some information for you,' she says. 'If you promise me you won't leave this bed again.'

It's not what I want. I want to see them for myself, know they are all OK. But if my body can't take me there, I'll settle for Donna finding out for me.

*

Donna returns to my room, with an air of caution around her.

She doesn't know much, but what she does know is that the woman in the car died at the scene. She'd lost too much blood; they couldn't resuscitate her. She couldn't find out any information about the twins other than they had to complete an emergency caesarean.

My chest feels like it's been stabbed, my heart torn out and thrown back in battered and bruised. My babies, could they have survived that? They weren't due yet, it's too early for them to survive. And Zoe … dead? No wonder Tom looked grief stricken. He thinks I've died. What if he thinks he's lost everything? Me *and* the twins. I can't bear the thought of him going through all that alone.

My parents must be devastated too. They will think it's me who died. All I want to do is reassure them, hold them and tell them I'm alive and that I love them.

Donna can see how distressed this has made me.

'See,' she says. 'This is why you didn't need to know, not right now anyway. It's not going to do you any good. I'm sorry, I should have stuck to my guns and not told you.'

'You know that wouldn't have worked,' I say. 'I needed to find out. If you didn't let me know, I'd have found out another way.'

'Look,' she says. 'I don't know what happened in that accident, but I'm pretty certain that you're not the kind of person to intentionally hurt someone. So, try not to feel too guilty about it all. Just focus on yourself for now, there's nothing else you can do.'

That's a lovely thing to say, but she hasn't got a clue. It's not guilt I feel, it's grief. But I can't tell her that.

'Thank you,' I say.

'Don't worry about it,' she replies. 'Now, we'll be having no more funny business please. I'm going to be keeping a close eye on you from now on. You're not going to be doing anymore Houdini's on me. I'll strap you in if I have to.'

There's no denying it anymore, I can't move from this bed. Physically my body has let me down and Donna will be keeping an extra close eye on me. All I can do right now is get better. Not for me, but for my family.

*

After a disturbed but much needed sleep, I wake to find Donna checking my machines.

'How long have I been sleeping for?' I ask her.

'You slept all through the night thankfully!' She says. 'You tossed and turned a lot, I kept thinking you'd wake up, but you didn't. It meant I could easily keep an eye on you, make sure you stayed in your bed. It's almost visiting hours now, so hopefully you'll get someone visit you. Put a smile back on that face.'

Well, I know that no-one would visit me, but Donna wouldn't expect that. I'm sure she'd think it strange that I'd have no visitors, especially after a serious accident like this. But then, she doesn't know the situation. Who knows, maybe it's more common than I think, for patients to be alone in hospital.

'I doubt it,' I reply, matter-of-factly. 'But it's OK, it's what I expect.'

I don't want Donna's pity. I know no-one will visit me, but not because I've done anything wrong. It doesn't warrant pity. It is what it is.

She bustles out of the room again to go and see her other patients. There's not a lot to do in hospital really. There's no TV unless you pay for it. All I have are a couple of tired magazines provided by the hospital. Therefore, I open one up and flick through the pages. It's all about the royal family and celebrities that I have no interest in, so dump it back on the bedside table.

There's a faint knock and the door of my room creaks open.

'Hello? Aish?'

It's Luke and Gemma and they're holding hands.

'Oh, look at you, you poor thing,' Gemma says. 'I know I've done a bad thing. And I know you probably don't want to see either of us, but I just couldn't stay at home, knowing what you'd been through.'

I look between the two of them. Gemma's holding a hold-all bag with one hand, and the other loosens from Luke's grip. Gemma remains focussed on me, but Luke's head is down, as if he can't bring himself to look at me.

'And you Luke?' I say. 'Why have you come?'

He slowly raises his chin but can't maintain eye contact. 'You know I loved you Aish. I never planned for this to happen with Gemma, but we have to get over it.'

'Oh, I'm over it Luke, you're welcome to each other. Although, I don't get why you're here.'

Gemma says, 'He came to support me. I needed to see you, to check you were OK. I've brought you a clean pair of

PJs, some clean clothes and some magazines. You're my best mate Aish, I've been so worried, you could have died.'

'Are you worried about me or the *other* Aish?' I reply. 'I *was* your best mate. Nothing's changed since our conversation in the card shop. And yes, I was in love with you too Luke, but things change. You've seen me now, I'm alive. You've made your peace, so there's no guilt to be felt. I suggest you toddle off together into the sunset and never come and see me again.'

'What? Did you … swap back?' Gemma's eyes widen in shock.

'It's none of your business now Gemma. As I said, you *were* my best mate and I'm done trying to prove myself to you. You betrayed me. Both of you did. Well, you're welcome to each other. I don't know why you decided to come. To rub it in my face no doubt.'

Luke swings his head up and stares directly into my eyes. 'I only came because Gemma begged me to …'

'Luke shhh …' Gemma interrupts. 'Let's just go. We shouldn't have come.'

She leaves the bag on the visitor's chair. 'Whatever you think of me right now, just know I really do care.' With that, they hurry back out of the room chattering to each other.

What irony. The last time I was in hospital, I longed for Luke and Gemma to be by my bedside. Instead, I had a strange man holding my hand called Tom, claiming to be my husband. Now, I've just ushered Luke and Gemma away from my bedside and what I wouldn't give to have Tom here holding my hand.

31

Shortly after Luke and Gemma leave, the door knocks again, so much for not having visitors.

'Zoe?'

My stomach flips. It's Mel.

'Oh my God, I'm so pleased you've come!' I say.

She doesn't look very happy. She pulls a chair up next to my bed and says, 'I'm not going to stay long. I'm just here to say one thing.'

She continues, 'Leave Tom alone now. He wants nothing more to do with you. And for that matter, you can stay away from me too. Do you have any idea what you've done?'

All I want to say is that it wasn't me. I want to grab her and hug her and tell her everything will be OK. She's clearly grieving and angry, understandably so. But she doesn't know we switched back and she certainly doesn't know that it's her sister that's died, not me.

'Mel, look, you need to know something,' I try to say.

'I don't want to know,' she says. 'I just need you to understand that the police will be questioning you. Tom's made allegations. You're looking at a murder charge Zoe. You've gone too far this time and hurt far too many people.'

'No, you don't understand ...'

'Yes, I do! You're selfish, manipulative and this time, no-one will be around to ...'

'We switched back!' I blurt out. 'We switched back.'

Confusion and shock sweep across Mel's face. 'What? No, no, no, I'm not falling for this.'

'Seriously, we did. I died at the scene of the accident, and I know Zoe did too. It's just this time, I found my way back to my body, but Zoe didn't.'

'But how do you know? How do you know she died?' Mel says.

'My nurse told me. All I've wanted to do since waking up is find Tom and the twins to explain. But the nurse wouldn't let me. She told me Zoe died in the accident. I'm so sorry. I know you had your bad times, but she was still your sister.'

'You're lying,' Mel says. 'That's all you ever do. Well, you know what? You may as well have died in the accident. You're dead to me. You hear? That's it, finished.'

With that she storms out of the room, leaving me sobbing uncontrollably into my pillow.

*

Sat on the edge of my hospital bed, I pack my few belongings into the hold-all Gemma left me, including my wallet which was found on me after the accident. Eight days I've been in this hospital and no-one else came to visit. Now it's time to go. But go where?

The last year has come full circle. On my own with no-one knowing who I really am. But this time, I'm stronger. I've done it before, and I can do it again. I need to get my family back, once and for all.

I'm still none the wiser about the twins. I have no idea if they survived or not. Donna wouldn't tell me anything more. She said she didn't know, but I don't think she would have said anything even if she did know.

The hospital ordered me a taxi which turned up promptly outside the main hospital entrance. I root around inside my wallet, there's a credit card and just enough pieces of shrapnel to scrape together a taxi fare.

The taxi pulls up outside the familiar, welcoming grey building. The hanging baskets are now full of new shooting spring buds, and the Bear Inn sign is cleaned and polished.

Arthur is stood behind his desk and welcomes me with his wrinkly smile.

'Good morning young lady, how can I help you?' He asks.

'Good morning,' I reply. 'I need a room please, just for a couple of nights hopefully.'

'Of course, my dear. Have you stayed here before? We have room four available, it's a quaint little room …'

'I don't suppose room two is available?' I ask. 'I know you keep it for special guests, but I've stayed there before, and it really is a wonderful room.'

Arthur looks a little baffled. 'You say you've stayed here before? I can't say I recognise you. Well room two is available and seeing as you asked so nicely, here's the key.'

Wonderful, I need as much familiarity as possible this time around. 'Thank you so much,' I say and wander up to my room for the night.

*

The morning spring glow lights up my room waking me from my much-needed slumber. The Nina Simone song, 'Feeling Good' plays in my head. It's a new dawn, it's a new day, it's a new life for me and I'm feeling good. I'm motivated and optimistic. It's time for me to get my life back together and plan for the future. Again.

There are people in my life that I need to reach out to in order to tell them my story. However, actually getting them to be in the same room as me, let alone listen to what I have to say, will prove difficult. There is only so much coincidence and impossibility people can believe.

My parents battled enough last time with believing my story that I have no idea where to start for a second time. It's one thing doing the impossible once in your life, let alone twice. I change bodies twice but can't expect them to believe me twice too.

As far as Mel is concerned, she thinks I'm her sister and hates me for what I've done. And as for Tom, he's also under the impression that I'm Zoe and caused the accident through jealously and revenge. There has to be a way to reach out and convince them.

There are ways I can prove my identity with my parents of course. I've done it before, and I'm sure I can do it again as we share so much history. But Mel and Tom are different. They don't know me for me very well. There's no history to draw on, nothing I would know about them that no-one else does.

This is the point that I decide there's only one thing that I can do, one way that I can tell them my story without them slamming a door in my face or telling me to go away.

*

'Morning, Arthur,' I say.

'Oh, morning young lady,' he replies. 'I hope you slept well. Beautiful morning isn't it? Summer's on the way!'

'Yes, thank you, I slept like a log,' I say. 'Um … Arthur, I know it's a little cheeky, but I don't suppose you have a computer here that I can borrow?'

I know full well he has his laptop but have no idea if he'll let me borrow it this time.

Arthur wrinkles his nose in a way that suggests he's not happy with me asking this. Perhaps he thinks I'm rude for asking. Perhaps he's taken a dislike to me.

'I'm sorry, it's rude of me to ask,' I say.

'Oh, not at all,' he replies. 'I do have a laptop, but it's getting very old and hasn't been working very well of late. I last lent it to another young lady. You remind me of her in some way. What is it that you need it for?'

'Oh, it's just to use the word processor programme, I need to write something.'

'Ah, no problem, it's just the internet that's dodgy. Will that be OK for you?'

'That's more than OK, thank you ever so much Arthur,' I say.

'Any time young lady, I'll bring it up to your room in a few.'

As promised, back in my room a few minutes later, Arthur knocks on my door with laptop in hand. I thank him, take it to the desk and start to write.

32

To Mum and Dad,

This is an exceptionally difficult letter to write as over the past year I have asked so much of you. There were some very dark times when I thought I would never have you back in my life again and now I am faced with the same possibility yet again.

My story is one that's so very hard to believe, even I sometimes struggle to trust that the events of the last year truly happened.

But know this, I have loved you both since the day I was born and will love you until the day I die. You see, I am your daughter. I'm not writing this to upset you both. I just don't want you grieving for a daughter that is very much alive.

I was involved in yet another tragic accident involving two cars, one with myself and Tom in and the other with Zoe in. Zoe overtook us and caused us to go into the back of her car.

She threatened me recently, saying that she would kill me if she had to in order to get her life back. I never told you both as I didn't want to worry you. But sadly, she ended up killing herself. You see, our souls switched again when we were both resuscitated at the scene of the accident. The only thing was that I found my way back to my original body, but she never did.

I haven't come to see you as I know it would be especially difficult for you to see me at this time, when you believe me to be dead. The last thing I want is to cause you any further distress. All I want is for you to trust in me and believe my story one last time.

You believed me before, and I have every faith that you will again. I'm here Mum and Dad, waiting for you. I'm staying at a little B&B called the Bear Inn. Please call or pop in and I'll make you both a cuppa with a bit of taste and fill you in on my unbelievable story.

I have also enclosed something else for you to read, which hopefully will help you understand what is going on and bring you back to me. I hope that you enjoy.

Please look after each other.

Much love as always,

Aisha

*

Dearest Mel,

Please believe me when I say this is not ideally how I would want to tell you my story. I tried to talk to you in hospital, but understandably you couldn't comprehend what I was saying.

Therefore, I am writing to you in the vain hope that you will read what I need to tell you. Please don't throw this away, please read it and then cast your own judgement. If you still feel the need to discard this letter after reading it, then that's your call. But I do hope you don't.

Growing up, I never had a sister but always wanted one. When I became part of Tom's life, I became part of yours and gained the sister I always longed for. You are a fantastic person. You're genuine, loving, funny and light up a room whenever you enter one. I am immensely grateful to have shared the short amount of time with you that I did and hope beyond all hope that this is not the end.

The sad news is that Zoe died in the accident. She was your real sister, and you need to grieve for her. I am not Zoe, I'm Aisha. It's hard to hear and I'm not saying this just to upset you, but you have lost her.

She got what she wanted. She did cause the accident and did cause us to switch back again. But what she wasn't counting on was her losing her life as a result. Yes, I hate her for what she did, but she deserves to be grieved for and you deserve that opportunity.

As a result of this letter, I hope that you realise the truth behind what happened and give your sister the send-off I know you would have wanted to.

I'm staying at a little B&B called the Bear Inn and would love to rebuild our friendship but understand if this is something you can't contemplate at this time.

To help you understand the last year better, I have enclosed something else for you to read. I hope you spend some time reading it and take what you can from it.

I'll be waiting to hear from you.

With love,

Aisha

*

Dear Tom,

I have spent the last two weeks writing. I've written letters to Mel and my parents, but this is the one that is by far the hardest to write.

There is so much that I have asked of you this last year, but I must make one more request and that is that you read this letter with an open mind and an open heart.

Forgive me for not meeting with you in person, but the way things are right now, I have no idea how to approach you and fear that it would be of detriment. These words are not meant to hurt you or cause pain, they are meant solely to tell you what happened and let you know that I love you.

Should you feel the need to contact the police after reading this, then I understand. Although, I do hope that you don't, not because I am scared but because I want you to believe that there is no need to.

It saddens me to know that you are currently under the illusion that I have died. I am very much alive, but without you and the twins, I may as well have died in that accident. At the same time, it also saddens me to know that you are grieving over the wrong person. Zoe died in that accident, not me. And for all her sins, she deserves to be grieved for.

The nurse in the hospital told me that Zoe and I both had to be resuscitated at the scene of the accident. Her plan worked Tom. We both died and switched back again. The only difference this time was that I was brought back but she wasn't.

The nurse couldn't tell me anything about the twins though, other than that the paramedics had to complete an emergency caesarean. Not knowing if they are alive is killing me. Not just so that I can grieve if they're not, but so that I know you're not on your own trying to deal with the loss of your wife and *your babies. I pray every night that the twins are safe and well.*

I understand this is not something easy for you to believe. God knows you've been through enough this year without me throwing this revelation at you. I'm not expecting you to believe me, but I hope you do. I miss you terribly and love you more than I've ever loved before.

Not only have I spent these last two weeks writing these letters, but I've also written something else which I've enclosed with this letter. It's an account of all the events of the last year from start to finish, on paper, my story and I've named it Junction. The name represents the scene of the accident but also symbolises the crossroads we've taken together and the crossroads of life and fate. I've sent copies to Mel and Mum and Dad to help them understand the events of last year. But it's your story just for you Tom in the hope that you'll read it and come back to me. The only thing that's missing from the book is the final chapter. For that I need your help Tom. I need to know how it finishes. Please let me know.

I love you and will always love you. I just hope that we can build a future together as planned. I'm staying at the same

B&B I stayed in before, called the Bear Inn. Please contact me.

With all my heart,

Aisha

Epilogue

My six o'clock alarm bleeps. Today is the eighteenth of July and the start of the rest of my life. There is so much to prepare and so little time. We have to be at the church by nine o'clock. There's a buffet to finalise, our outfits to iron and gifts to wrap.

By eight-fifty-five we arrive at the church, just in the nick of time. The graveyard is full of beautiful daisies with dandelions sporadically spotting the scene. It's a beautiful, sunny summer's day. Walking up to the big oak door I feel overwhelmed with emotion when I hear the organ playing *Toccata and Fugue in D Minor* by Bach.

I place our card box on the table inside the Church porch. It's a beautiful white celebratory box made of cardboard with a little letter-box hole in the top. This will save family and friends from having to carry their cards with them throughout the service.

Inside we wait for our guests to arrive and listen to the haunting sounds of the organ pipes bellowing air through them.

My parents are the first to arrive and take a pew behind me. I turn around as they shuffle in behind me and both mum and dad plant kisses on my cheek before sitting down on the cushioned bench.

Mel arrives next with her new boyfriend Aaron. Arm in arm they walk down the aisle and take a pew to my left. I smile at her and she waves frantically back at me with a broad smile sweeping across her face, oozing excitement.

Gradually the church fills with other distant family members.

The church is decorated with beautiful pink, red and yellow flowers creating a lovely floral air around me.

At this moment, the events of the last year are wiped from my memory and all I can think of is the future. Our future, together.

Whilst staring at the altar with a childish grin on my face a hand squeezes my right thigh bringing me back from my daydream.

'Today's the day,' Tom says with an equally childish grin on his face. 'We made it.'

We did indeed.

A baby cries, Tom reaches into a bag and pulls out a brightly coloured rattle. Another baby cries, so he reaches in and grabs a soft cuddly bear.

He gives me the bear to comfort Livia and keeps the rattle for him to comfort Eva. They're grouchy after the manic morning preparing for their big day. They don't understand why everyone around them are the happiest they've ever been. But one day, when they're older they will.

We named them Eva and Livia because, like my name, both names mean life. They are both miracles of life and have given us all a new meaning to ours. But the strangest thing I noticed when trawling through baby names with Tom, is that Zoe also means life.

'Thank you all for gathering here today,' the vicar says. 'Today we welcome the families of Eva and Livia who will be Christened today. We will be welcoming them both into the Church and invite you all to stay for a coffee after the service.'

We made it. Through thick and thin, Tom read my story and believed me.

*

After our family and friends enjoy their coffee and biscuits, they all start to leave the church to make their way to a village hall we hired for the afternoon celebrations.

Tom offers to take the girls back to the car and get them snuggly strapped into their car-seats whilst I gather up our belongings. He places a kiss on my lips and pushes the dual pram through the big oak door.

I grab the twins' bags and toys and almost forget to pick up the card box on the way out of the church.

Bizarrely, as I turn to grab the card box, there is a card in a pink envelope left on the top of the box with no writing on the front. It's completely blank but sealed. How odd. I contemplate posting it through the letter-box hole and opening it later along with the rest of the cards, but curiosity gets the better of me. I put down the bags and open it.

It's not a Christening card. Instead, it's a very plain white card with 'Thinking of You' written in bold, blue font across the centre of it. I peel back the front page feeling a surge of dread sweep through my chest. Inside, scrawled in familiar writing, it reads quite simply, 'Still Ticking …'

Out of the corner of my eye I see a shadow move in the graveyard. I turn and squint to try to make out the figure that's distorted by the sun's glare. The sun is too bright but as I scrunch my eyes and put my hand above my head as a sunshield, I can just make the shadowy silhouette of an arm moving slowly, yet meaningfully, toward the figure's forehead. My eyes gradually focus on the index finger and widen as it continues to move firmly and menacingly toward my direction.

To Be Continued …

Acknowledgements

I had a dream. Quite literally. So, firstly, I would like to thank my unconscious mind for giving me the foundation for my first novel.

My parents, John and Bethan, I thank you for being the most amazing parents I could ask for. You proofread and gave me the advice and support I needed.

A big thank you goes to my best friend, Georgie, for giving me inspiration and notable suggestions which I listened to and used in the final version of 'Junction - Time's Ticking'.

My biggest thanks go to Carl. For having belief in me when I didn't always believe in my own ability. For supporting me and suggesting ideas. For encouraging me to finally finish the book and urging me to publish. Without your love, reassurance and insight, 'Junction – Time's Ticking' would still be a half-written word document saved on a dusty laptop.

My gratitude also goes to all those who took the time to read 'Junction – Time's Ticking' draft, after draft, after draft and offering feedback and support.

The Junction Trilogy

L. A. Evans

Junction: Time's Ticking

Junction: Still Ticking

Junction: Time's Up

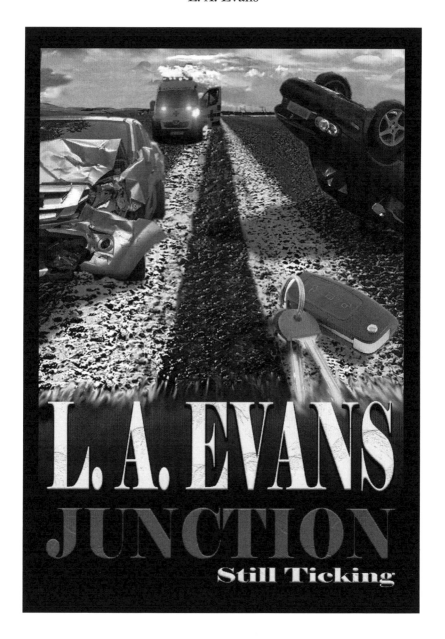

Junction
Still Ticking

L. A. Evans

Follow Zoe on her path towards redemption in this sequel to *Junction: Time's Ticking*. Find out what makes this self-obsessed, controlling, deceitful woman tick. Why is she so set on destroying Aisha Brown's new life and so determined to reclaim it as her own?

There are always two sides to every story. What horrors did Zoe encounter on her journey and what nightmares await? Was death her destiny all along or did fate have something far more sinister planned?

A dark insight into her life before and after her world collided with Aisha's. Many mysteries from *Junction: Time's Ticking* will be revealed. Including who or what Aisha saw in the graveyard on that sunny, celebratory summer's day.

This second thriller in *The Junction Trilogy* will take you on a chaotic ride. Buckle in and brace yourself for a disturbing insight into the chilling life of Zoe Young.

Watch out for side roads. Don't let them pass you by.

Please be advised, this book is intended for adults and contains mature content.

Printed in Great Britain
by Amazon